John Kent

Eternal Burning

A scandal against the Almighty

John Kent

Eternal Burning
A scandal against the Almighty

ISBN/EAN: 9783337410292

Printed in Europe, USA, Canada, Australia, Japan

Cover: Foto ©Andreas Hilbeck / pixelio.de

More available books at **www.hansebooks.com**

Eternal Burning

A SCANDAL

AGAINST THE ALMIGHTY.

By JOHN KENT.

TRENTON, N. J.:

MacCrellish & Quigley, Printers, 16 E. State St.

1880.

PREFACE.

By presenting this to the world the author purposes to show that the doctrine of Eternal Burning does not belong to the Divine Word; and that, although the intrinsical immortality of man was, even in Bible times, believed and taught by all other nations, the Jews, the people of God, did not believe in the immortality of man, except through the resurrection; and, also, that Christ and His Apostles taught and proved that upon the resurrection only, depended the future existence of those who had passed away.

Furthermore, the author purposes to show, independently of all the argument that is generally presented in opposition to Eternal Torment, that there is no ground for such a doctrine. He purposes to show that the evidence adduced to sustain this doctrine, is ample, of itself, not only to condemn it, but also to prove the contrary; and, that the evidence against it, aside from this, is overwhelming, and not only to the effect that such a doctrine is contrary to the realities of the Scriptures, but that it is a Scandal against the Almighty.

INTRODUCTION.

The doctrine of Eternal Burning has become so firmly rooted in the mind of man, that all the sects of Christendom, with few exceptions, whilst claiming to worship the Almighty as a God of Justice, of Mercy, and of Love,—a God Who so loved even fallen—sinful humanity, that He gave His only begotten Son to die for them, teach that He is a God of Insatiable Vengeance, Whose wrath nothing but the Eternal Burning of the wicked in a Lake of Fire and Brimstone can appease. They teach that He is never satisfied with punishing them, for they are always being punished; and that the narrowest limit to His Vengeance is, having them always Burning in Hell.

This I pronounce a damnable heresy, and claim, as the Scriptures teach, that Death is the result of Sin,—that the punishment of Sin is Death, and that the Everlasting Death will be the Everlasting Punishment; that the First Death is the result of Adam's sin, and that the Second Death will be the result of each sinner's own sins. "For as in Adam all die, even so in Christ shall all be made alive."

"IN ADAM ALL DIE." This is the First Death, the result of the first transgression. Yet, "IN CHRIST SHALL ALL BE MADE ALIVE;" and then the question will be settled as to who shall live the Second, or Eternal Life, and who shall die the Second, or Everlasting Death.

Now, be it remembered and ever kept in view, that upon the assertion that Death is not Death, is based this unholy doctrine of Eternal Burning in a Hell of Fire and

Brimstone. For, in the face of the Scriptures to the effect that the Second Death shall be the last of the wicked, the Advocates of Eternal Burning assert, with the greatest audacity, that it will not be a Death at all, but an Eternal Life. Yea, according to their teaching it will be an Eternal Life, by far, more momentous than the Eternal Life of the Saint. Yes, were it. true, that which they teach as the punishment of the wicked would be ten thousand times more to be dreaded than the reward of the Saint is to be desired.

But now that those passages which are presented as teaching or supporting the idea of an Eternal Burning of the wicked in a Hell of Fire and Brimstone, may come before the mind in all their glowing brilliancy, I have gathered them together, and assure the reader that, though he may regard them as favoring the idea of Eternal Torment, if he will lay aside prejudice, and with me, follow the current of Divine Truth, he shall see that the blinding blaze of Eternal Burning vanishes from sight; and that, instead of Insatiable Vengeance being an attribute of God, such teaching is a Scandal against Him.

So now, while prejudice and falsehood grasp each other's hand, while bigotry sneers with brainless contempt, and blind sectarianism staggers on its way, let us face this question in its unclothed reality, and let the Scriptures decide for all.

ETERNAL BURNING

A

SCANDAL AGAINST THE ALMIGHTY.

Now, commencing with Matthew, XXVth chapter, at
31st verse, we read:

"When the Son of man shall come in his glory, and all
the holy angels with him, (but not before,) then shall he sit
upon the throne of his glory: And before him shall be gathered all nations: and he shall separate them one from
another, as a shepherd divideth his sheep from the goats:
And he shall set the sheep on his right hand, but the goats
on the left. Then shall the King say unto them on his
right hand, Come, ye blessed of my Father, inherit the Kingdom prepared for you from the foundation of the world:
For I was a hungered, and ye gave me meat: I was thirsty,
and ye gave me drink: I was a stranger, and ye took me
in: Naked, and ye clothed me: I was sick, and ye visited
me: I was in prison, and ye came unto me. Then shall the
righteous answer him, saying, Lord, when saw we thee
a hungered, and fed thee? or thirsty, and gave thee drink?
When saw we thee a stranger, and took thee in? or
naked, and clothed thee? Or when saw we thee sick, or
in prison, and came unto thee? And the King shall answer
and say unto them, Verily I say unto you, Inasmuch as ye
have done it unto one of the least of these my brethren, ye
have done it unto me. Then shall he say also unto them
on the left hand, Depart from me, ye cursed, into everlasting
fire, prepared for the devil and his angels: For I was a hungered, and ye gave me no meat: I was thirsty, and ye gave

me no drink: I was a stranger, and ye took me not in: naked, and ye clothed me not: sick, and in prison, and ye visited me not. Then shall they also answer him, saying, Lord, when saw we thee a hungered, or athirst, or a stranger, or naked, or sick, or in prison, and did not minister unto thee? Then shall he answer them, saying, Verily I say unto you, Inasmuch as ye did it not to one of the least of these, ye did it not to me. And these shall go away into everlasting punishment; but the righteous into life eternal."

Here we have the two facts upon which the whole question rests, squarely presented before us. The righteous shall enter into Life Eternal, but the wicked shall go away into Everlasting Punishment.

When, therefore, all shall have been assembled before the bar of judgment, and the wicked, then, and there, condemned and sentenced, the only thing remaining will be the execution of that sentence; and hence the saying, " These shall go away into everlasting punishment."

This points us to the XXth chapter of Revelation, 14th and 15th verses, where is shown the spot where this sentence will be executed, and the manner in which it will be done:

"And death and hell were cast into the lake of fire. This is the second death. And whosoever was not found written in the book of life was cast into the lake of fire." Hence we see that the sentence which will be pronounced upon the wicked, at the judgment, will be executed by their being cast into the lake of fire, which, though we are called upon by the fallacious to believe will constitute an Eternal Life, the Apostle declares, "is the Second Death." And so conspicuously does the ascription of Eternal Life to the righteous display the difference between them and the wicked, that we cannot fail to see that the wicked shall suffer that Perishing which those who believe on the Son of God will escape, through the gift of Eternal Life.

The present Life of the Saint is Temporal, but the next will be Eternal. The Death which the sinner dies here, is but for a time, but the Second Death will be Everlasting. If all shall live Eternally, why talk so much about Eternal Life? If the wicked, as the righteous, shall live Eternally, this talk about Eternal Life is not consistency. Therefore, to make it appear that the wicked and righteous both live Eternally, reduces this particular discrimination of the Scriptures which ascribes the Second, or Eternal Life to the one, and the Second, or Everlasting Death to the other, to nothing other than foolishness; which, however, it is evident, is the best they can do in favor of the terrible cruelty with which they charge the Divine Being.

WHERE THE BEAST AND THE FALSE PROPHET ARE.

But now we will turn to the XIXth chapter of Revelation; and that we may embrace all that bears upon the subject, commence at the 19th verse: "And I saw the beast, and the kings of the earth, and their armies, gathered together to make war against him that sat on the horse, and against his army. And the beast was taken, and with him the false prophet that wrought miracles before him, with which he deceived them that had received the mark of the beast, and them that worshiped his image. These both were cast alive into a lake of fire burning with brimstone. And the remnant were slain with the sword of him that sat upon the horse, which sword proceeded out of his mouth : and all the fowls were filled with their flesh." How significant the phrase, " Cast into a lake of fire burning with brimstone"? How plainly it shows that they were destroyed? It is equivalent to saying that they were not destroyed with the sword, but that, seemingly more terrible, they were captured alive, and then destroyed in a lake of fire and brimstone.

But, say the Advocates of Eternal Torment, They were not destroyed, for the next chapter teaches the contrary. This, no doubt, will be the general cry; for this phrase, " Where the beast and the false prophet *are*," is a central pillar of their fabric of Eternal Torment. But while they consider me bold for saying they were destroyed, they had best pause a moment and see if they stand upon so sure a foundation as they might at first suppose. For, beginning at the 7th verse of the XXth chapter, we read: "And when the thousand years are expired, Satan shall be loosed out of his prison, And shall go out to deceive the nations which are in the four quarters of the earth, Gog and Magog, to gather them together to battle: the number of whom is as the sands of the sea. And they went up on the breadth of the earth, and compassed the camp of the saints about, and the beloved city: and fire came down from God out of heaven, and devoured them. And the devil that deceived them was cast into the lake of fire and brimstone, where the beast and the false prophet *are*, and shall be tormented day and night for ever and ever."

This, as all must see, covers the whole ground, and presents the truth in its simple reality. Yet, in all this, there is but one word that conflicts with the foregoing assertion, and, that *it* may appear in its most conspicuous form, I will again repeat the verse in which it is contained: "And the devil that deceived them was cast into the lake of fire and brimstone, where the beast and the false prophet *are*,* and shall be tormented day and night for ever and ever."

In this verse are presented two facts, which, though particularly distinct, are, nevertheless, confounded by those who are particularly anxious to perpetuate the doctrine of Eternal Burning. For the torment spoken of in this verse,

---

Are is the word referred to.

is particularly confined to the devil; for, "The devil that deceived them was cast into the lake of fire and brimstone, where," it is said, "the beast and the false prophet *are*, and shall be tormented day and night for ever and ever."

Now, if John had intended to convey such an idea as that the wicked should be tormented as the devil was, Why did he not say that the devil that deceived them, and all whose names were not found written in the book of life, were cast into the lake of fire and brimstone, and should be tormented day and night for ever and ever? Surely, if he had intended to convey such an idea, he would have thus expressed it! But no; having no such an idea to convey, he tells us that the devil shall be punished for ever and ever; and then, after telling us all that he knows about torment for ever and ever, he tells us what shall become of the wicked; that is, he tells us that they shall be punished with the Second Death by being cast into the lake of fire. Therefore, this being tormented day and night for ever and ever, is the punishment which will be inflicted upon Satan only, who is a supernatural being; and, being such, we cannot determine as to what amount of punishment he shall receive, though it be for ever and ever in a Lake of Fire and Brimstone. But if the doctrine that, at death, the wicked are sent to a Hell of Fire and Brimstone be correct, and that the devil is there as Head and Chief, and can exist in, and enjoy such a place for six thousand years, certain it is that his change of residence shall not amount to much, notwithstanding the for ever and ever.

But how ridiculous, and how false does this fact, that the devil shall be punished in a lake of fire and brimstone, make the teaching of those who tell us that the wicked are suffering, and the devil rejoicing in a Hell of Fire and Brimstone? Surely, as the former is positively true, the latter is positively false!

Now, having thus separated the devil from humanity, and shown that it is not mankind, but he only, who "shall be tormented day and night forever and ever," the question rests with the beast and the false prophet. For, say they, "The devil was cast into the lake of fire and brimstone, where the beast and false prophet are." But this is a bold assertion; this is a sandy foundation to build so lofty a fabric upon; for the translators have not told us that the original said, "Where the beast and the false prophet are," but they have put in the italics, and have thus shown us that it was not, "Where the beast and the false prophet are," but that it was something else. When, therefore, we remember that "the wicked shall be punished with everlasting destruction from the presence of the Lord, and from the glory of his power," we see that this something else, was—*were cast into.* Therefore we see that the devil was cast into the lake of fire and brimstone, into which the beast and false prophet had been cast; that is, (as all the facts connected with the case prove,) he was cast into the lake of fire and brimstone, in which the beast and the false prophet had been destroyed.

But it seems that, seeing that it conflicted with the doctrine of Eternal Burning, the translators, instead of giving us the original, have, for it, as the italics show, substituted *are;* and this is the best evidence that they could have given us to the contrary of *are;* for it is emphatically to the effect that the original was not—"Where the beast and the false prophet are;" which leaves it clearly positive that it was, Where the beast and the false prophet had been destroyed. Therefore we see, that instead of these passages which are held up as teaching Eternal Burning in the Flames of Hell, accomplishing such an object, they utterly condemn the same. They not only do not prove that the erring of humanity shall be Eternally Burned in a Blazing Hell, but, if there were no other evidence to prove the contrary, they show the utter falsity of this doctrine, and indicate the corrupt source whence it originated, and the deceitful channel through which it has flown.

TORMENTED WITH FIRE AND BRIMSTONE.

In XIVth chapter, 9th and 10th verses, it is said: "And the third angel followed them, saying with a loud voice, If any man worship the beast and his image, and receive his mark in his forehead, or in his hand, The same shall drink of the wine of the wrath of God, which is poured out without mixture into the cup of his indignation; and he shall be tormented with fire and brimstone in the presence of the holy angels, and in the presence of the Lamb." True; and terrible torment it will be, just as the torment of those of whom the world was not worthy, was terrible torment, when they were sawn asunder, any more than that, if possible, it will be more terrible. For, just as those martyrs were tormented in the presence of cruel men by being sawn asunder and thus killed, these, their murderers and the like, when cast into the lake of fire, will be tormented in the presence of the holy angels, and in the presence of the Lamb, just as they had tormented the righteous in this life.

And how plainly does it appear that the tormenting of the wicked will be, as was that of the martyrs, confined to a time, simply sufficient to accomplish their destruction? For who could suppose that the holy angels and the Lamb shall stand for ever and ever witnessing the torment of the wicked? Surely, all must answer, none! And so it is manifest that those who shall be tormented by being cast into a Lake of Fire and Brimstone, shall live for ever and ever, no more than those who were sawn asunder, who could not have lived for half an hour.

FOR EVER AND EVER.

Again, the Word says: "The smoke of their torment ascendeth up for ever and ever." And how positively does this confirm the truth as taught by the Psalmist; that is, that "the wicked shall consume," that "into smoke shall they consume away"? It positively reiterates his assertion.

Now, concerning the consuming of this mighty mass of humanity, the Apostle said "the smoke of their torment ascendeth up for ever and ever," just as was common to say, "O, king, live for ever," or, "Long live the king." Hence, just as for ever denoted a long life, as in the case of the king, so, for ever and ever was applicable to the complete consuming of this ponderous mass; that is, as in the case of the king, for ever meant live long, it meant smoke long in this. Hence, when the various ways in which the phrase, for ever, was used, are taken into consideration, the fact is obvious that for ever meant the time required to accomplish a work or object, which time, though indefinite and long, always terminated when the work was done, or the object accomplished. Not that a long smoking was as long as a long life, but that live for ever, meant live long, and that smoke for ever, meant smoke long.*

Again, after describing the last scene first, which, and similar were common with Scriptural writers. John describes that which had happened very remote from this; that is, he goes back to time, and tells us that "those who worship the beast, have no rest day nor night," just as the Prophet had said concerning such, long before. For Isaiah had said: "There is no peace, saith my God, to the wicked;" which is

---

*With regard to the phrase, For ever, the reader should remember that what it meant when used by the Prophets, by Christ and the Apostles, is what is to be accepted as its meaning in the Scriptures, notwithstanding that it is made to represent a different idea at the present day. For, though we say, for ever, and mean without end, it does not make the for ever, of the Bible, mean differently from what it meant in the days of Moses and the Prophets.

but a slight difference of phraseology in expressing the same fact.

Then the writer connects this with the 12th verse, and says: "Here is the patience of the saints; here are they that keep the commandments of God, and the faith of Jesus?" When had they the patience? Why, in the first life. When did they keep the commandments of God, and the faith of Jesus? Why,—but is it necessary to answer? Who that has knowledge enough to make him responsible, cannot see that it was among those who worshiped the beast, and their like—those wicked ones who had no rest day nor night? And who, therefore, cannot see that instead of this supporting the doctrine of Eternal Burning, it clearly establishes the truth as declared by the Psalmist, that "the wicked shall perish, and the enemies of the Lord shall be as the fat of lambs;" that "they shall consume;" that "into smoke shall they consume away"? Whether they will see or not, they shall, "They shall," says David, "consume; into smoke shall they consume away."

"THEIR WORM DIETH NOT."

In Mark, IXth chapter, 43d and 44th verses read thus: "And if thy hand offend thee, cut it off: it is better for thee to enter into life maimed, than having two hands to go into hell, into the fire that never shall be quenched: Where their worm dieth not, and the fire is not quenched." But the fact that "the fire is not quenched," has no bearing upon the nature of the punishment of the wicked, as denoting continuation of punishment,* for the fire was prepared for the devil and his angels, and therefore, all that

---

*This term, Quenched, however, has much to do with the punishment of the devil; and, inasmuch as "all Scripture is . . . profitable," and, at least, should not be

is left for consideration, is the phrase, "Their worm dieth not."

Here we see that they are not the worms, but that it is, "*their worm.*" Therefore "their worm" means their punishment, and the fire that "is not quenched," is the means by which they shall be punished. "Their worm" does not mean them, any more than their punishment means them, but their worm and their punishment are one and the same.

But, in reference to this question, Isaiah has preceded; and therefore, this is but, as it were, a quotation from him. But, then, what of the prophet? What has he said in regard to this matter? Best would it be to answer: Let us see.

His declaration is this: "They shall go forth, and look upon the carcasses of the men that have transgressed against me: for their worm shall not die, neither shall their fire be quenched; and they shall be an abhorring* unto all flesh."

Now, if Isaiah had been a teacher of Eternal Burning, surely he would have said: "Look upon the *Spirits* of the men that have transgressed against me, and hear their wails and groans while suffering the Torment of Burning Flames." But no! And how positively the opposite: "Look upon the *carcasses* of the men that have transgressed against me." Far does he put this doctrine of Eternal Burning from him, and positively does he confirm

---

misunderstood, it is proper to have a correct idea of his punishment, notwithstanding that it will be so very different from that of humanity's.

The phrase, "Never shall be Quenched," though held up in so frightful a form by the Advocates of Eternal Burning, constitutes, nevertheless, quite a modification of their doctrine, even as regards the punishment of the devil, for, to Quench, means to totally extinguish. Therefore, though "the fire never shall be quenched" until the object for which it was or shall be created, shall have been accomplished, it could be slackened to any extent whatever; and therefore, to the devil, who is a supernatural being, the torment spoken of may prove to be ten hundred million times less punishment than that which the Advocates of Eternal Burning so eagerly and earnestly proclaim as the offspring of Divine Justice, cherished and held in store for erring humanity, by a God of Love.

*The righteous will behold them, as David says, consuming into smoke. A sickening sight will it be; and therefore, an abhorring unto them.

the preceding, when he says: "They shall look upon the *carcasses* of the men that have transgressed against me."

And now, having sifted the fact from the phraseology, it will be seen that the phrase, "Their worm dieth not," simply denotes their Everlasting Death. For were it so that a man could be punished by being deprived of life for one day, the punishment would cease at the end of the day, and he would live again; and if he were thus punished for a year, the result would be the same at the end of the year. But were he sentenced to unlimited death, the punishment would be Everlasting; and therefore his punishment would not cease, notwithstanding that he were destroyed for ever; for this being destroyed for ever, would be his punishment.

THERE SHALL BE WEEPING AND GNASHING OF TEETH.

I shall now give attention to a part of the XIIIth chapter of Luke, commencing at the 24th verse: "Strive to enter in at the strait gate: for many, I say unto you, will seek to enter in, and shall not be able. When once the Master of the house is risen up, and hath shut to the door, and ye begin to stand without, and to knock at the door, saying, Lord, Lord, open unto us; and he shall answer and say unto you, I know you not whence ye are: Then shall ye begin to say, We have eaten and drunk in thy presence, and thou hast taught in our streets. But he shall say, I tell you, I know you not whence ye are; depart from me, all ye workers of iniquity. There shall be weeping and gnashing of teeth, when ye shall see Abraham, and Isaac, and Jacob, and all the prophets, in the kingdom of God, and you yourselves thrust out."

Here, in the 27th verse, we see that the workers of iniquity will be commanded to depart; and, in 28th verse, we see that "there shall be weeping and gnashing of teeth,

2

when they shall see Abraham, and Isaac, and Jacob, and all the prophets, in the kingdom of God, they themselves thrust out."

If this passage did not show an interval between their being cast out, and their final destruction, that might be overlooked, it would not be of importance enough to require particular notice, in connection with the subject of Eternal Torment. For, in reality, it amounts to nothing more than their giving of vent to their agony upon realizing their utterly lost condition, when commanded to depart as the workers of iniquity.

Now, that " there shall be weeping and gnashing of teeth, when they shall see Abraham, and Isaac, and Jacob, and all the prophets, in the kingdom of God, and they themselves thrust out," surely, is nothing strange! For who would not weep and gnash their teeth, when once they were certain that they should be destroyed in a lake of fire and brimstone ? Yea, who would not! And will not such destruction be terrible enough ? Surely, it will! And the fact is obvious that there will be plenty of time between the command to depart, and the final destruction, for this weeping and gnashing of teeth.

So, as all that is mentioned in connection with this matter, precedes their being cast into the lake of fire, we see that all that this weeping and gnashing of teeth has to do with Eternal Burning, exists in the misled minds, or in the evil hearts of its advocates.

THE RICH MAN AND LAZARUS.

In compliance with the arrangement which I have determined upon, that is, of fairly confronting all the passages that are held up as teaching Eternal Torment, I now turn to the XVIth chapter of Luke; and shall, before proceeding to the consideration of any part of it, record all of the last paragraph of that chapter.

"There was a certain rich man, which was clothed in purple and fine linen, and fared sumptuously every day: And there was a certain beggar named Lazarus, which was laid at his gate, full of sores, And desiring to be fed with the crumbs which fell from the rich man's table: moreover the dogs came and licked his sores. And it came to pass, that the beggar died, and was carried by the angels into Abraham's bosom: the rich man also died, and was buried; And in hell he lifted up his eyes, being in torments, and seeth Abraham afar off, and Lazarus in his bosom. And he cried, and said, Father Abraham, have mercy on me, and send Lazarus, that he may dip the tip of his finger in water, and cool my tongue; for I am tormented in this flame. But Abraham said, Son, remember that thou in thy lifetime receivedst thy good things, and likewise Lazarus evil things: but now he is comforted, and thou art tormented. And besides all this, between us and you there is a great gulf fixed: so that they which would pass from hence to you cannot; neither can they pass to us, that would come from thence. Then he said, I pray thee therefore, father, that thou wouldst send him to my father's house: For I have five brethren; that he may testify unto them, lest they also come into this place of torment. Abraham saith unto him, They have Moses and the prophets, let them hear them. And he said, Nay, father Abraham: but if one went unto them from the dead, they will repent. And he said unto him, If they hear not Moses and the prophets, neither will they be persuaded, though one rose from the dead."

Having thus presented before the reader the passage as recorded in Luke, I shall first proceed with the consideration of it, as regards the accepting of it in a literal sense.

The kind of discoursing seen in the 22d verse, is not uncommon in the Scriptures; and that which is there stated is intended, simply to call the mind to that which is still future. For, according to the literal sense of the language, dead Lazarus, not his spirit, had been taken by the angels to Abraham's bosom; where, according to 23d verse, the Rich Man had seen him in immortal bloom; whilst 31st verse says that for him to have testified to the brethren of the Rich Man, he would have needed a resurrection from the dead. Therefore we see the bungling strategy connected with the idea of construing the passage so as to present a present reality of things.

Twenty-fifth verse: "But Abraham said, Son, remember that thou in thy lifetime receivedst thy good things, and likewise Lazarus evil things; but now he is comforted, and thou art tormented." This, accepted in a literal sense, is just as positively to the effect that for no other reason than that he had enjoyed the good things of this life for a few years, the Rich Man had been consigned to the torments of hell, as it is positively asserted, taking it literally, that "in hell he lifted up his eyes, being in torments." But what a wretched picture to represent the character of God! What! consign the Rich Man to the Flames of an Eternal Hell, and Lazarus to Eternal Happiness, simply because the one had had much that the other had not earned a penny of, and the other had had nothing, yet had not been robbed of a farthing by the other? Such an act would not contain even a spark of justice. Ten thousand times worse would it be than ten thousand times ten thousand Rich Men could be capable of! Yet, if the passage were literal, this would be the only reason there could be given for doing it; or rather, for its having been done. So, one being as positively literal as the other, the blackened character that a literal acceptation of it would give to God, should make even the Advocates of Eternal Burning shrink with horror from such an application of it.

Now, I shall review the passage—not in the light of, or, rather, the darkness of Eternal Burning, but in the light of God's Word.

The first of the paragraph, the 19th verse, says: "There was a certain rich man, which was clothed in purple and fine linen, and fared sumptuously every day." This, accepted in a figurative sense, which is the only Scriptural sense in which it can be accepted, might very correctly be construed to represent a different class from those to which I shall, at present, apply it, and which I am satisfied are the great objects of the text.

Yes, this might well be quoted as representing the Clergy generally of the present day, for they are clothed in equivalent to purple, and in fine linen, and fare sumptuously every day, whilst many who are called upon to assist in thus supporting them, are so indigent that themselves and all around them manifest nothing but poverty.

But passing this, the passage, from the 19th to the 21st verse, simply represents the two extremes, wealth with all that it can impart, and poverty in its lowest grade.

Twenty-second verse: "And it came to pass, that the beggar died, and was carried by the angels into Abraham's bosom: the rich man also died, and was buried." It would be impossible—according to any doctrine, to accept this language as literal, for the beggar died; and—not the spirit, but the dead beggar, taking it literally, was carried by the angels into Abraham's bosom. Therefore, taken in its proper sense, we see that it points to that time, when, or shows us that there will be a time, when the angels will carry, even resurrected beggars to share eternal felicity with faithful Abraham, in the everlasting kingdom, as shown in Matthew, XXIVth chapter and 31st verse: "And he shall send his angels with a great sound of a trumpet, and they shall gather together his elect from the four winds, from one end of heaven to the other."

Now, Why should God want to gather them, or how could He gather them "from one end of heaven to the other," whilst they were all with Him in heaven? The Advocates of Eternal Burning may tell why, and how, as they do many other things; but common sense will still look at the text, and say: Why should He, or how could He gather them?

Twenty-third verse: "And in hell he lifted up his eyes, being in torments, and seeth Abraham afar off, and Lazarus in his bosom." Here, again we are forced to accept the language in a figurative sense, for it says: "In hell he lifted up his eyes, being in torments." Did it say, "In hell he lifted up his eyes," omitting the torment, it might more consistently be construed as literal; but inasmuch as it embraces torment, and, as the following verse shows, in flame, it cannot be construed as anything other than figurative, directing the mind to the final destruction of the wicked in the lake of fire, the only hell in which there is said to be (Scripturally) a reality of burning.

We here read of the rich man's being in hell, after he had died, and had been buried. Jonah was in hell; and, as regards this hell, there can be no mistake, for he told God that he had been in hell, and God has never, even indirectly, contradicted it.

So now, leaving the figure, we will, by turning to Revelation, XXth chapter, take a full view of the fact. "And I saw the dead, small and great, stand before God; and the books were opened." What were they opened for, to see how many hundred years the wicked had been Burned in Hell? Were they opened to see whether or not they had suffered the pains of Burning Flames long enough to be judged? The Advocates of Eternal Burning may answer, yes; and to carry out their direful doctrine they must. But God's Word tells quite a different story, for it says: "And the dead were judged out of those things which were written

in the books, according to their works;" that is, at the
judgment; but never before will they be judged, rewarded,
or punished.

But we return to the question, Hell. "And the sea gave
up the dead which were in it; and death and hell delivered
up the dead which were in them: and they were judged
every man according to their works." Here we see another
hell—not a hell of the living, as was Jonah's, but of the
dead; and in the 14th and 15th verses we see that death,
and hell, and all the wicked were cast into the lake of fire.
Not the Spirits of the dead, but the dead; for it was the sea
that had held the dead, and death that had held them, and
in company with these, hell also had held them; and they,
with the resurrected wicked, the sea excepted, are represented as being together destroyed, after the last resurrection and the judgment, in the lake of fire, the only hell in
which a Burning is represented as being a literal reality.
Therefore the situation of the Rich Man, as shown in Luke,
must, in part, be regarded as typical of the terrible destruction pictured in the foregoing.

Twenty-fourth and twenty-fifth verses: "And he cried
and said, Father Abraham, have mercy on me, and send
Lazarus, that he may dip the tip of his finger in water, and
cool my tongue; for I am tormented in this flame. But
Abraham said, Son, remember that thou in thy lifetime
receivedst thy good things, and likewise Lazarus evil
things: but now he is comforted, and thou art tormented."
Equal measure is represented and taught by this—Lazarus
desired the smallest favor possible of the Rich Man, and, as
is evident, was refused it—the Rich Man desired the
smallest favor, and he, in turn, was refused it; which shows
that "the measure that we meet, shall be measured to us
again." But what could be more foreign to justice and
truth than the direful doctrine that when " the measure that
they meet, shall be measured to them again," that, for the

wrongs which they have done, as in the case of the Rich Man, they shall not only be deprived of life and forever cut off from the land of the living, but shall be consigned to Eternal Burning in the Flames of Hell, by One who himself is humanity; whilst also "God knoweth our frame, and remembereth that we are dust!"

Twenty-sixth verse: "And besides all this, between us and you there is a great gulf fixed: so that they which would pass from hence to you cannot; neither can they pass to us, that would come from thence." This shows that the two classes, the one represented by the Rich Man, and the other by Lazarus, will be for ever separated. But taken in a literal sense, in connection with the three preceding verses, it shows that those who are, by the Advocates of Eternal Burning, represented as being in perfect happiness, are always witnessing the inexpressible misery of their unfortunate friends—perhaps parents, brothers, sisters, or all three, or more, in the Flames of Hell. Hence, to accept the language as figurative is the only way that we can do justice to its Author.

The following verses give us to understand that we shall not seek unto the dead, but unto the Lord. They show us that if we want to know anything about the other side of the grave, we shall go to God's Word, which is more reliable than the word of any one would be, who might rise from the dead, who, of course, would know nothing, as will hereafter be made manifest.

Thirty-first verse: "And he said unto him, If they hear not Moses and the prophets, neither will they be persuaded, though one rose from the dead." No, they would not have been persuaded though Lazarus had risen from the dead! But according to the teaching of those who claim the immortality of man independently of the resurrection, Lazarus was then in all the vigor of immortality, and why should not he have been sent, without a Resurrection? It needs no answer! It would be nonsense, yea, even crime, to connect a literal signification with this passage, and therefore it is manifest that there is no present reality about it.

THE 37th AND 38th VERSES OF THE XXth CHAPTER OF LUKE, AND THE 28th VERSE OF THE Xth CHAPTER OF MATTHEW.

Now, I shall continue by turning to the XXth chapter of Luke, 37th and 38th verses, that, by properly analyzing them, a clear understanding may be had of that passage which is so often presented as the grand palladium of the doctrine of Eternal Burning, the 28th verse of the Xth chapter of Matthew: "And fear not them which kill the body, but are not able to kill the soul: but rather fear him which is able to destroy both soul and body in hell." But, commencing with the first mentioned passage, we read: "Now that the dead are raised, even Moses showed at the bush, when he called the Lord the God of Abraham, and the God of Isaac, and the God of Jacob. For he is not a God of the dead, but of the living: for all live unto him."

In order the better to simplify the foregoing, (for it is not only complex, but also very abstruse,) I shall here answer, as well as ask, a number of questions; and commence by saying: Who showed "that the dead are raised?" Why, Moses showed it. When did he show "that the dead are raised?" Why, "when he called the Lord the God of Abraham, and the God of Isaac, and the God of Jacob;" that is when he showed it. What did Moses show at the bush? Why, he showed "that the dead are raised." But how did he show "that the dead are raised?" Why, he showed that the dead are raised, by calling the Lord the God of Abraham, and the God of Isaac, and the God of Jacob; that is how he showed it. But for what reason did he show by this, "that the dead are raised?" Why, because "God is not a God of the dead, but of the living: for all live unto him."

Now, as this shows that the dead are raised, so it shows that there are dead to be raised; and therefore it shows that when a man dies he ceases to exist, and is not a being for God to be a God of. Yet, when the body is killed or the man dies and the soul ceases to exist, his existence does not cease; for whether good or bad, God has decreed that he shall exist again. And as there are those who are dead, and yet all live unto God, and this is what shows that "the dead are raised," the reason why all live unto Him, is because He can, and will call them forth at His pleasure. For just as surely as Moses, by calling the Lord the God of Abraham, and the God of Isaac, and the God of Jacob, had shown that "the dead are raised," so surely Jesus showed that the dead live unto God because—and only because He can, and will call them forth at His pleasure. Hence, when the body is killed and the soul ceases to exist, it is not; and as God is not a God of that which is not, but of that which is, and of those who are, and of those who shall be, He is not a God of the dead, but of the living.

But when God says that "the soul that sinneth, it shall die," He means that it shall die the Second Death, when both soul and body shall be destroyed in the lake of fire, which destruction will be for ever. For God is able to destroy both soul and body in hell, and plainly shows us that if we do not fear Him, we shall, in this manner, be destroyed.

Hence He has given us to understand that the existence of the soul does not depend upon the natural life, but that it depends upon His word, or calling; and that, inasmuch as He can call them forth at His pleasure, they all live unto Him, though they be killed, and so cease to exist for a time; and that, as all live unto Him, though men kill the body, they cannot kill or destroy the soul as unto Him; for that, unto Him it lives, and shall live until both soul and body shall be destroyed in the lake of fire, after which it shall live no more, there being no resurrection thereafter; and that, as all live unto Him until that time, the soul cannot be destroyed before that time; for that, notwithstanding that the soul ceases to exist, its existence does not cease; for it must exist again, just as it first existed, and then, if of the wicked, be destroyed for ever, and exist no more.

And the fact is obvious that, no matter when it is done, the soul is first destroyed, and then the body; for as soon as the life is gone, the soul is destroyed; for then nothing remains but the inanimate man, and when this is destroyed, though the whole living being is the soul, the soul and body are both destroyed; for this being, a soul, which embraces all that living humanity is, cannot be a soul when the life is gone which makes a soul of it. Hence, when the life is gone, the soul is destroyed, though the body still remain to be destroyed.

Again, we see that, when Christ said, "Fear not them which kill the body, but are not able to kill the soul," He spoke with reference to two existences; and of course we take it for granted that He knew what a soul was, and that, what the Holy Word tells us it is, that that is what Christ knew it to be. So, beginning with Adam, we see that God made man of the dust of the ground, and breathed into his nostrils the breath of life, and that, then, man became a living soul; and that, therefore, that which he was after the breath of life had been breathed into him, which was nothing more nor less than a soul, is what Christ knew a soul to be. He knew that Noah, Job, Daniel, and all the descendants of Adam were souls; and He knew that the organic structure and the breath of life was what, and all that constituted a soul. Therefore He knew that when the body was killed and the breath of life, called the spirit, went forth, the soul, for a time, ceased to exist. Yet He said, "Fear not them which kill the body, but are not able to kill the soul."

So now, let us compare this with what is said in Ezekiel; that is, "Behold, all souls are mine; as the soul of the father, so also the soul of the son is mine: the soul that sinneth, it shall die." Now, suppose that some one had killed that soul that sinned, it would surely have ceased to exist just as the one referred to by Christ when he said, "Fear not them which kill the body, but are not able to kill the soul." Yet, notwithstanding that it would have ceased to exist for a time, that which God had spoken concerning it would not have been fulfilled. Therefore, when Christ said, "Cannot kill the soul"—the self, He meant, could not destroy its existence hereafter, just in accordance with what God meant when he said, "The soul that sinneth, it shall die;" that is, die the Second Death. For all must die the first death, whether good or bad, but the wicked must die the Second Death; for the soul that sinneth, though, through the first death, it ceases for a time to exist, it must exist again; and, as God has decreed, die the Second Death. Therefore, though God simply says, "The soul that sinneth, it shall die," the import of it is, that, although the wicked die the first death, it will not relieve them from the punishment which He has decreed; that is, that they shall die the Second Death. Hence we see that, when Jesus said, "Fear not them which kill the body, but are not able to kill the soul," He meant, "Fear not them," who, though they terminate this life, cannot deprive you of an existence hereafter; for though you cease to exist for a time, you still live unto God; for He can, and will call you forth at His pleasure. Therefore, as the first death of the soul that sinneth cannot relieve Him from the punishment of the Second Death, so the suffering of the first death cannot deprive the saint of the Second, or Eternal Life, which will be his reward.

Now, as this is so plainly and positively to the effect that the dead are dead, and that the reason why the dead live unto God is because He can, and will call them forth at His pleasure, How plainly and how positively does it condemn the worse than heathenish story concerning the Eternal Burning of the erring of our race, in a Hell of Fire and Brimstone? How plainly does it show that just as surely as Christ meant anything when he said, "Fear not them which kill the body, but are not able to kill the soul: but rather fear him which is able to destroy both soul and body in hell," He meant that, if they did not fear Him, they should thus be destroyed; and that, therefore, He meant just what David, His father according to the flesh, meant, when he said, "The wicked shall perish, and the enemies of the Lord shall be as the fat of lambs: they shall consume; into smoke shall they consume away!" It confirms this fact, and makes it as positive that the Second Death will be the last of the wicked, as it is positive that Christ uttered the words: "Destroy both soul and body in hell." For Christ has shown that the body of the wicked shall be destroyed in hell, (the lake of fire,) and He has just as clearly shown that, then, the soul will have ceased to exist.

THE PASSAGES YET TO BE NOTICED.

With respect to the passages yet to be noticed as favoring the immortality of man independently of the resurrection, the question will not be merely what they are, *but are they what they should be,* as well as what they are.

Now, as all must realize that the Divine Word cannot be other than harmony, the love of truth should compel us to receive it in its unclothed reality; and that it may thus be seen and understood, I shall take the liberty of rejecting, as the imperfections of humanity, a few items, which, in the light of this same Divine Word, none could receive, though he even desired to do so. And, reader, when, through the better feelings of our nature and the more expanded reachings of the mind, we are enabled to surmount the barriers that bigotry, infatuation, and designing apostates have reared upon the highway of holiness, we can easily see that the love of truth is the only qualification necessary to fit us to determine the question with regard to these passages, which are four in number, and all of the same class.

THE SPIRITS OF JUST MEN MADE PERFECT.

In Hebrews, XIIth chapter, 23d verse, we find the phrase, "The spirits of just men made perfect." But it is evident that, in the original, it was not, "The spirits of just men," but the Spirit of just men made perfect, which Spirit, is the Holy Ghost; or, that it was, To the Spirit by which you have been made perfect; for there is no perfection in or connected with death; it is all imperfection. But the Spirit, the Holy Ghost, is that by which we are made perfect. For God justifies them that believe in Jesus, and then they are just, and then they are made perfect by the Holy Ghost that is given unto them, by which the love of God is shed abroad in their hearts; and then they are the just men made perfect by the Spirit, without which they could not be perfect. Therefore it requires no more than a genuine Christian experience to make one capable of understanding the original, in the place of which, we have this phrase.

THE BOOK OF LIFE, AND THE BOOK OF LIFE OF THE LAMB SLAIN FROM THE FOUNDATION OF THE WORLD.

I shall now consider two passages conjointly.

In Revelation, XXth chapter, 4th verse, we find it written : " And I saw the souls of them that were beheaded for the witness of Jesus, and for the word of God." But before proceeding further with this, I shall record the 8th verse of the XVIIth chapter, which reads thus : " The beast that thou sawest was, and is not; and shall ascend out of the bottomless pit, and go into perdition : and they that dwell on the earth shall wonder, whose names were not written in the book of life from the foundation of the world, when they behold the beast that was, and is not, and yet is."

Here it is affirmed that " they shall wonder, whose names were not written in the book of life *from the foundation of the world.*" Therefore the idea conveyed is, that the names of those who should be saved, had been written in the book of life thousands of years before they were in existence; and that all others had been, at the same time, doomed to destruction; which is as foreign to the original, the Divine Word, as darkness is to light, as is shown in the 8th verse of the XIIIth chapter, " And all that dwell upon the earth shall worship him, whose names are not written in the book of life *of the Lamb Slain* from the foundation of the world."

It is manifest therefore, that, instead of their names having been written in the book of life from the foundation of the world, they had been written in the book of Jesus Christ, Who was " the Lamb of God" that had been foreordained as a provision in behalf of man, before the foundation of the world. Therefore it is not only the book of life, but the book of life *of the Lamb Slain* from the foundation of the world. Hence we see that, for whatever reason, the phrase, *of the Lamb Slain*, has been omitted in the XVIIth chapter; and looks as though it had been done by design, in favor of the immortality of man, without a resurrection.

Now, turning to the XXth chapter, we have a case parallel with that of the XVIIth, the difference being, that whilst in the 8th verse of the XVIIth chapter, the phrase, *of the Lamb Slain*, has been omitted, the 4th verse of the XXth chapter has been interlarded with, *of them*. But now we will read the passage, and then determine as to this peculiar feature:

" And I saw thrones, and they sat upon them, and judgment was given unto them: and I saw the souls of them that were beheaded for the witness of Jesus, and for the word of God, and which had not worshiped the beast, neither his image, neither had received his mark upon their foreheads, or in their hands; and they lived and reigned with Christ a thousand years. But the rest of the dead lived not again until the thousand years were finished. This is the first resurrection. Blessed and holy is he that hath part in the first resurrection: on such the second death hath no power, but they shall be priests of God and of Christ, and shall reign with him a thousand years."

This represents John as saying that he saw—not the persons who had been beheaded, but the souls of those persons; and that then he says those souls lived and reigned with Christ a thousand years; and then again, that he says that the rest of the dead lived not again until the thousand years were finished. This, as all must plainly see, is the reality of the passage with the phrase, *of them*. But what nonsense this, *of them*, makes of the whole passage? What sense could be made of such a bungling, contradictory arrangement? And who cannot see that the phrase, *of them*, is the cause of all this confusion, and that, therefore, no matter how it got there, it does not belong to the Divine Word?

But now, reader, omitting this foreign element, you will see how harmoniously all the facts unite and prove that this, *of them,* did not belong to the original, and that the passage is the Divine Word without it, thus: " And I saw thrones, and they sat upon them, and judgment was given unto them : and I saw the souls . . . . that were beheaded for the witness of Jesus, and for the word of God, and which had not worshiped the beast, neither his image, neither had received his mark upon their foreheads or in their hands; and they lived and reigned with Christ a thousand years. But the rest of the dead, (that is, dead souls,) lived not again until the thousand years were finished. This is the first resurrection. Blessed and holy is he that hath part in the first resurrection : on such the second death hath no power, but they shall be priests of God and of Christ, and shall reign with him a thousand years."

In all this, is there a single word that conflicts with another? No. There is not a shadow of discord. The passage throughout, is perfect harmony.

When Christ was on earth, He promised His Apostles, that, " In the regeneration, when the Son of man should sit upon the throne of his glory, they should sit upon twelve thrones, judging the twelve tribes of the children of Israel." In the 4th verse of the preceding, John says: " I saw thrones, and they sat upon them, and judgment was given unto them." Here they are in the regeneration, and the promise fulfilled, but not until after the first resurrection.

In the beginning, God made man of the dust of the ground, and then, after He had thus made him, He breathed into his nostrils the breath of life and man became a living soul. Therefore, a soul is what Adam was, and all his descendants are souls. They can be nothing more nor less in this life; they can be nothing more nor less in the future.

John, therefore, in speaking of the resurrected righteous, says: "I saw the souls . . . . that were beheaded for the witness of Jesus, and for the word of God;" that is, he saw that those righteous persons who had been beheaded, (they being the most prominent characters,) with all the rest of the righteous, lived and reigned with Christ a thousand years; during which time the wicked were still dead, as they, the righteous, had been, before they were resurrected.

So now, as it is manifest that the passage with, *of them*, is nothing but discord, and even contradicts the teachings of those who teach it, it is certainly manifest that this, *of them*, instead of belonging to the Revelation of Jesus Christ, belongs to the apostates who invented it. And therefore we see that this passage, instead of favoring the doctrine of a Burning Hell between Death and the Resurrection, confirms the truth as taught by Paul, that, in the absence of the resurrection, all had perished.

THE WORD BRING.

Now, lest any should suppose that the Scriptures ought to be received, as many teach, in the absence of reason, I take the liberty of asserting the contrary, and of assuring the reader that, relying upon the reality of the Divine Word, he need not fear, though he here find, as in the preceding, defects in the work of its translators. And so, turning to 1st Thessalonians, IVth chapter, we find that it requires but a small amount of reason, and but ordinary common sense, to remove all difficulty in regard to the future state, so far as the last of these passages is concerned.

This passage, with its surroundings, I now record : " But I would not have you to be ignorant, brethren, concerning them which are asleep, that ye sorrow not, even as others which have no hope. For if we believe that Jesus died and rose again, even so them also which sleep in Jesus will God bring with him. For this we say unto you by the word of the Lord, that we which are alive and remain unto the coming of the Lord shall not prevent them which are asleep. For the Lord himself shall descend from heaven with a shout, with the voice of the archangel, and with the trump of God: and the dead in Christ shall rise first: Then we which are alive and remain shall be caught up together with them in the clouds, to meet the Lord in the air: and so shall we ever be with the Lord. Wherefore comfort one another with these words."

There is not a word in the New Testament that is more clearly to the contrary of the original, from whatever cause, than the word *bring*, in the 14th verse of the foregoing. This word, surrounded as it is with such plain, such comprehensible facts, looks as though it had been placed there for the purpose of supporting the immortality of man to the · exclusion of the fact that upon the resurrection only, depends his future existence. For Paul had in view the comforting of those who had friends who were in their graves; and lest they should have supposed that those friends would be left behind when the Lord gathered IIis Church, the word "bring" excepted, he said: "But I would not have you to be ignorant, brethren, concerning them which are asleep, that ye sorrow not, even as others which have no hope. For if we believe that Jesus died and rose again, even so them also which sleep in Jesus will God bring with him."—1st Thessalonians, IVth chapter, 13th and 14th verses.

Now, if they had been in heaven, or where God was going to take the living, why would God bring them with Him ? If they had been in heaven in perfect safety, Why should Paul have comforted the living concerning them ? If they had been safe when God was going to take the living, the living would have needed no comfort concerning them, for they would have been the safer of the two. But if comfort had been needed by either party, under such circumstances, it would have been needed by those who were in perfect safety; they would have needed comfort concerning those who had not yet escaped that danger from which they had been safely delivered. Hence, how plain the fact that the word *bring*, in our present copies, was TAKE, in the original?

Again, when, in the 14th verse, we read that " them also which sleep in Jesus will God *bring* with him," we can see how flatly this *bring* is contradicted by the following verses, thus : " For this we say unto you by the word of the Lord, that we which are alive and remain unto the coming of the Lord shall not prevent them which are,"—What! Awake, mingling in the triumphant shout of the coming lost? No; but "asleep." For the Lord himself shall descend from heaven with a shout, with the voice of the archangel, and with the trump of God: and the dead in Christ shall rise first. Now, how harmoniously does this unite with the declaration of Jesus to the effect that the time should come when those who were in their graves should hear His voice and come forth? But who would not blush to hear one say, They shall be raised from heaven to earth? And yet, if they be brought, instead of taken, this is the only process, which, of course, is as absurd as the declaration. Hence it is manifest that *bring* does not belong to the Divine Word, but that it belongs to the advocates of the heretical doctrine of inborn immortality; and that it has been substituted for TAKE, through actual infatuation, or willful design.

But how plain do all the facts appear, and how harmoniously are they all united, when *bring*, which undoubtedly did not belong to the original, is removed, and TAKE occupies its place? For, with this construction, we can see why we should be comforted; for we shall be taken up to meet the

Lord in the air, and we have friends who are asleep, or in their graves, we do not want to have them left behind; it would be a source of the greatest discomfort, to think that when we shall be taken from the sorrowful scenes of earth, those loved ones who are in their graves should be left behind. This, Paul very well knew, and the contentions about the resurrection had made this question about the case of the dead, one of the greatest importance; and therefore, he said: "I would not have you to be ignorant, brethren, concerning them which are asleep, that ye sorrow not, even as others which have no hope. For if we believe that Jesus died and rose again, even so them also which sleep in Jesus," will He raise from the dead, and TAKE with Him. "For this we say unto you by the word of the Lord, that we which are alive and remain unto the coming of the Lord shall not prevent them which are asleep. For the Lord himself shall descend from heaven with a shout, with the voice of the archangel, and with the trump of God: and,"—What—Shall the living saints descend? No; "the dead in Christ shall rise." "For the Lord Himself shall descend from heaven with a shout, with the voice of the archangel, and with the trump of God: and the dead in Christ shall rise first: Then we which are alive and remain shall be caught up together with them in the clouds, to meet the Lord in the air: and so shall we ever be with the Lord."

Now, it is manifest that, by the use of the word *bring*, the translators tell us that the dead are in heaven; and that, then they tell us that they are asleep; and that, then they tell us that they shall be brought from heaven; and then again, that they shall be raised out of their graves, prior to being taken to heaven. Therefore, if they had left this word with the heathenish doctrines, where it belonged, and given us that which undoubtedly the original was, TAKE, we should not have been troubled with this discordant mass, but would now have the original, the Divine Word to the effect that, though so many of Christ's followers are in their graves, there is not one forgotten. "For the Lord himself shall descend from heaven with a shout, with the voice of the archangel, and with the trump of God: and the dead in Christ shall rise first: Then we which are alive and remain shall be caught up together with them in the clouds, to meet the Lord in the air: and so shall we ever be with the Lord." And we should be able to comply with Paul's exhortation: "Comfort one another with · these words."

But who could understand such comforting as *bring* would make! Yet how comprehensible and how comforting, when we accept the passage as it is evident the Apostle wrote it, that, "If we believe that Jesus died and rose again, even so them also which sleep in Jesus will God" TAKE "with Him?" It is equivalent to saying: My beloved Thessalonian brethren, if you believe that Jesus Christ our Lord died and rose again, rest assured that your friends who have died in this precious faith, shall not be left behind when the Lord comes to take you. For He Himself, Who is the resurrection and the life, will, as He has said He would, call them forth from the grave, their resting-place, and you shall together be taken from the then chaotic scene, until the earth, having passed through its fiery ordeal, shall be returned to its Eden purity and loveliness and fitted for the everlasting abode of the ransomed. This is the import of it all, and how easily understood, and how exceedingly comforting!

Now, as this is so clearly to the effect that the grave is the resting-place of the saint, between death and the resurrection, that they all sleep as Lazarus slept, and that, as he was called forth, they shall be called forth, the direful teaching to the effect that the wicked are in a Blazing Hell, between death and the resurrection, is forced from the face of the Sacred Volume; and finds its level, if its level can be found, only among those Damnable Heresies, which, by the apostates, were brought into the Church.

SAMUEL, SAUL, AND THE WITCH OF ENDOR.

And now, inasmuch as some have presented the case of Saul and Samuel, recorded in 1st Samuel, XXVIIIth chapter, to prove that man exists in a future state independently of the resurrection, or rather, as it should be said, independently of himself, I call the reader's attention to the contents of the chapter, so far as bears upon this subject, and that, as ever, we may have the facts before us in their plain form, we will commence at the 7th, and read to the 19th verse.

" Then said Saul unto his servants, Seek me a woman that hath a familiar spirit, that I may go to her, and enquire of her. And his servants said to him, Behold, there is a woman that hath a familiar spirit at Endor. And Saul disguised himself, and put on other raiment, and he went, and two men with him, and they came to the woman by night: and he said, I pray thee, divine unto me by the familiar spirit, and bring me him up, whom I shall name unto thee. And the woman said unto him, Behold, thou knowest what Saul hath done, how he hath cut off those that have familiar spirits, and the wizards, out of the land: wherefore then layest thou a snare for my life, to cause me to die? And Saul sware to her by the Lord, saying, As the Lord liveth, there shall no punishment happen to thee for this thing. Then said the woman, Whom shall I bring up unto thee? And he said, Bring me up Samuel. And when the woman saw Samuel, she cried with a loud voice: and the woman spake to Saul, saying, Why hast thou deceived me? for thou art Saul. And the king said unto her, Be not afraid: for what sawest thou? And the woman said unto Saul, I saw gods ascending out of the earth. And he said unto her, What form is he of? And she said, An old man cometh up; and he is covered with a mantle. And Saul perceived that it was Samuel, and he stooped with his face to the ground, and bowed himself.

"And Samuel said to Saul, Why hast thou disquieted me, to bring me up? And Saul answered, I am sore distressed : for the Philistines make war against me, and God is departed from me, and answereth me no more, neither by prophets, nor by dreams: therefore I have called thee, that thou mayst make known unto me what I shall do. Then said Samuel, Wherefore then dost thou ask of me, seeing the Lord is departed from thee, and is become thine enemy? And the Lord hath done to him, as he spake by me: for the Lord hath rent the kingdom out of thine hand, and given it to thy neighbour, even to David: Because thou obeyedst not the voice of the Lord, nor executedst his fierce wrath upon Amalek, therefore hath the Lord done this thing unto thee this day. Moreover the Lord will also deliver Israel with thee into the hand of the Philistines: and to-morrow shalt thou and thy sons be with me: the Lord also shall deliver the host of Israel into the hand of the Philistines."

Here we see that, Saul and his servants having gone to the woman by night, Saul desired her to divine unto him by the familiar spirit, and bring him up whom he should name. Now, reader, be careful to observe, as you proceed; what is taught by the conversation between these parties, for, as stated above, Saul desired the woman to divine by the familiar spirit, and to bring down,—Is that right? No. But why not? If Saul had believed that Samuel was in heaven, down would be correct. But, according to the reality of the case, down is certainly wrong; for, said Saul, "Bring me him up whom I shall name unto thee." Hence we must understand that he believed Samuel to be in the grave, and that it was thence he expected the woman to bring him. We also see that she did not say, Shall I bring one from hell, from purgatory, or, shall I bring one down from heaven? No; but said she, "Whom shall I bring *up* unto thee?" But why did not Saul tell her that he had made a mistake, that she could not bring him up, for he was in heaven, and that, therefore, she would have to bring him down? If there had been a shadow of such an idea connected with the case, we might wonder why he did not tell her so, but as it is, there is no need of wonder, for he understood the question, and expressed his desire in full, when he said: "Bring me *up* Samuel."

Now, where did this, or this so-called Samuel come from? Could I have made a mistake in regard to the idea conveyed by the request of Saul and the answer of the woman? Let us see. "And when the woman saw Samuel, she cried with a loud voice: and the woman spake to Saul, saying, Why hast thou deceived me? for thou art Saul. And the king said unto her, Be not afraid: for what sawest thou? And the woman said unto Saul, I saw gods ascending out of the earth." But why did they not come from heaven, where all the righteous are located by those who teach that the wicked, between death and the resurrection, are suffering in the Flames of Hell? Let the answer be what it may, the coming of these gods, or of this god, was out of the earth.

Then said Saul: "What form is he of? And she said, An old man cometh up; and he is covered with a mantle. And Saul perceived that it was Samuel, and he stooped with his face to the ground, and bowed himself."

So now let us see what Samuel had to say about where he came from.

"And Samuel said to Saul, Why hast thou disquieted me," —Job, when speaking of rest in the grave, said: "I should have lain still and been quiet, I should have slept: then had I been at rest." Yes; and just so Samuel had been at rest, before he was disquieted. But Samuel did not only say, "Why hast thou disquieted me?" but said he: "Why hast thou disquieted me, to bring me up?" So Samuel said that he had been disquieted, and that he had been brought *up*. It was *up* that Saul had requested the woman to bring him, and it was out of the earth that he had expected him to come. And having, as he had expected he would, found the Prophet just what he had known him to be before his death, without a whisper concerning the glories of heaven or the torments of hell, he said: "I am sore distressed; for the Philistines make war against me, and God is departed from me, and answereth me no more, neither by prophets, nor by dreams: therefore I have called thee, that thou mayst make known unto me what I shall do."

Then Samuel answered. But did he say that what he had prophesied concerning Saul and the kingdom of Israel was confirmed by what he had seen and heard before the throne of God in heaven, where the Fabulists say he had been from the time of his death? Not so much as the remotest intimation of such a thing did he give, but said: "Wherefore then dost thou ask of me, seeing the Lord is departed from thee, and is become thine enemy? And the Lord hath done to him, as he spake by me: for the Lord hath rent the kingdom out of thine hand, and given it to thy neighbour, even to David: Because thou obeyedst not the voice of the Lord, nor executedst his fierce wrath upon Amalek, therefore hath the Lord done this thing unto thee this day." And then, as though to establish forever, as indisputable, the facts that there was neither a heaven nor a hell, for either himself, or for Saul, between death and the resurrection, but that their rest would be in the dust, he said: "Moreover the Lord will also deliver Israel with thee into the hand of the Philistines: and to-morrow shalt thou and thy sons be with me."

Now, no matter what opinions there may be in regard to the contents of this chapter, one fact stands out, isolated and prominent; that is, that Saul, his companions, and the woman, all believed that Samuel and the rest of the dead were in their graves; that they were not to be brought from heaven, from hell, nor from purgatory, but that, if communicated with, they were to be first raised *up* out of the earth. Therefore, that which has come from Endor as the voice of Samuel, utterly condemns as being a Damnable Heresy, the direful dogma of Eternal Burning; for, referring to the grave, to Saul he said, "To-morrow shalt thou and thy sons be with me."

THE OTHER SIDE OF THE QUESTION.

Now that all the passages of importance that seem to favor the doctrine of Eternal Burning, together with many that are regarded as more particularly favoring the intrinsical immortality of man, have been fully quoted and faced in their reality, and have been found to prove that, instead of Eternal Burning being the destiny of the erring of humanity, the Second Death, and it only, is their destiny, What may we expect when we come to examine the other side of the question? Why it follows as an inevitable result, that, as the evidence adduced to sustain it, proves the contrary, those passages which are more clearly to the contrary, must sweep even the last tint, or rather, taint of this noxious falsity from the face of the Sacred Volume.

But before proceeding further, the mind of the reader should be refreshed with regard to the doctrine in question; for it has become so common to say, Eternal Punishment, Eternal Hell, Everlasting Torment, and the like, that the real nature and magnitude of this arrangement concerning the erring of humanity, are seldom realized. But now, reader, as nearly as possible, you shall have this doctrine before you, in its plain form.

Lest, however, any should suppose that in the preceding or following, injustice is done to those who teach Eternal

Torment, be it understood that the punishment which they teach, cannot be magnified. It is not within the power of man to produce more terrible ideas than are connected with the doctrine of Eternal Torment. Therefore, reader, rest assured that, be it described as it may, its terribleness can never be told.

This doctrine is positively to the effect that all who fail to comply with the requirements of the Gospel, are, at death, consigned to the Flames of Hell; that there, in that unceasing Torment of Fire and Brimstone, their punishment is carried on by Satan and his host, (fire-proof beings,) who, by so doing, are, as his willing servants, executing the decree of the Almighty. And that, although the wicked, at the judgment, (according to their doctrine,) will have been Burned in Hell, some, for five or six thousands of years, they shall be brought forth to trial; that then the question of guilt will be determined, and that, then, they shall be punished.

But how criminally false is this doctorine! Mark it, thousands of years of punishment in Flaming Fire to precede the Judgment! Who that does not close his eyes to the light of God's Word, and to all that reason dictates, can fail to see that they have laid aside the plain truth, and embraced a most execrable lie? And how utterly repugnant to every true believer, yea, and to every one else who does not love falsehood better than himself, should this apostate, this popish, this worse than heathenish story of a Burning Hell between death and the resurrection, appear.

Again, when we read in God's Sacred Volume that He hath appointed a day in the which "he will judge the world in righteousness by that man whom he hath ordained," and again, that, after the last resurrection, "the books shall be opened, and that another book shall be opened, which is the book of life, and the dead shall be judged out of those things which are written in the books, according to their works,"

What more should be required to make a Christian blush, than to be told that the diabolical heresy of Eternal Burning in a Blazing Hell had been taught in the past! and how degrading for him to mention it as true, or countenance its being taught in the future!

COMMENCEMENT OF THE SO-CALLED ETERNAL PUNISHMENT.

Now that the question so far as punishment for six thousand years in the Blazing Fire of a Literal Hell, prior to the Resurrection and Judgment, has been fairly considered, I shall, though still continuing the evidence connected with the subject as prior to the Judgment, endeavor to give an idea of this doctrine, as subsequent to that event; for that which they teach as preceding the Judgment, being limited by time, is not Eternal Punishment.

This direful story concerning the punishing of the wicked, after the last resurrection, which, in reality, is the doctrine of Eternal Burning, represents the Almighty as having made extraordinary use of His wisdom to prepare and to perpetuate a punishment for the erring of humanity, so terrible, that, although the punishment described in the foregoing is ten thousand times ten thousand times greater than God's Word declares that the punishment of the wicked shall be, when compared with it, it is found to be—not as a drop to a bucket, but as one to the mighty ocean. For this doctrine of Eternal Burning is to the effect that after the Judgment, the wicked shall be "Cast into the lake of fire and brimstone, prepared for the devil and his angels;" and that, there, in that Burning Hell, they shall be punished; that, though they Burn in that Literal Flame for a hundred years, a God of Justice cannot be satisfied with such punishment. They must continue to Burn. And that, though such horrid pangs be endured for a thousand years in the presence of a God of Mercy, there can be no mitigation. They must still continue to Burn in that Blazing Hell. Yea, that when ten thousand years shall have been added to the other, even a God of Love cannot stay His hand. O Damnable Heresy! But thanks be to God that such teaching is not mine!

Yet it does not stop here; for ten thousand years of punishment added to a thousand, is but, as it were, a beginning. I have heard it described and taught thus, that, "If the Allegheny Mountains were to be removed by a bird that would come once in a thousand years and carry off a pebble, the time that would be required to accomplish the work, would not be Eternity; and that, therefore, such a length of time would not end the sufferings of the wicked, in the Flames of Indescribable Torment.

Alas! poor erring humanity! How they can lift their eyes towards heaven and attribute such work to the Almighty, is surely amazing beyond measure! I almost tremble while describing it as being charged against Him, and I should fear the destruction of the damned, were I to charge Him with the ten thousandth part of such cruelty!

God is Just, and Justice is His severest attribute. He is Merciful; yea, He is a God of Love. For, although man had sinned and incurred the penalty of death, " God so loved the world, that he gave his only begotten Son, that whosoever believeth in him should not perish, but have everlasting life." What a change in the picture! Instead of God combining all His powers to invent and carry on a punishment which would suit, though not satisfy the Insatiable Vengeance which the Advocates of Eternal Burning ascribe to Him, His powers have been concentrated in order to save us from the punishment of the Second Death.

LIFE AND DEATH.

Now that we have life and death before us, let us for a while examine, that we may see what the realities of these things are. The Advocates of Eternal Burning tell us that Life means Life, and then they tell us that Death means Life too. But now mark the difference between the wise man, and those who teach Eternal Burning. Says Solomon, "The living know that they shall die." Certainly, say the Spiritualists, we all know that we shall die, but death is only the gateway to Everlasting Life, and as soon as death removes the fleshy vail from our immortal eyes, we shall know all that we know now, and thrice as much more; for our knowledge will embrace the rapturous scenes of the region of glory. But stop! Let us hear the rest of his story; for he does not only say, "the living know that they shall die," but says he: "The dead know not anything."

Here we see that the difference between Solomon, and those who teach that death is the gateway to eternal felicity, is, that the Inspired one emphatically asserts that "the dead know not anything," and that the others tell us that they know all that humanity, mortal or immortal, can know. Hence we see how positively contrary to the Scriptures, is their teaching in regard to the wicked; for were they in a Hell of Fire Burning with Brimstone, it is certain that Solomon's declaration would be false. Therefore we see that, as Solomon's assertion is the reality of the Scriptures, the teaching to the effect that the wicked are Burning in Hell, is a fabrication of man; which leaves the reality just as the Inspired one has declared it to be; that is, that "*the dead know not anything.*"

Now let us see if this corresponds with what Job understood the reality of Death to be. But why say *if!* for says he: "Man dieth and wasteth away: yea, man giveth up the ghost, and where is he?" Then he tells us where he is; for says he: "As the waters fail from the sea, and the flood decayeth and drieth up; so man lieth down, and riseth not." But, say the Spiritualists, they are rejoicing in heaven. Yet Job continues: "Till the heavens be no more, they shall not awake, nor be raised out of their sleep."

Here, again we see the difference between the realities of the Scriptures, and the fabrications of man. The Scriptures teach us that when man dies, he is as the flood that decayeth · and drieth up; that is, that he is not—does not exist. But the Fabulists tell us that the wicked of them, are in a Hell of Fire Burning with Brimstone. The Scriptures tell us that, "till the heavens be no more they shall not awake, nor be raised out of their sleep." The Fabulists tell us that the righteous of them, are not only awake, but are rejoicing most gloriously, in heaven, and that they never were asleep. They represent the dead Christian as being in the vigor of immortal bloom; with his mind expanded, his thoughts reaching out and embracing all that can be brought within the scope of that intellect with which his immortal self, through the blessing of death, has been crowned with. But ah! how differently David looked at Death! Said he, when looking at this event which the Fabulists describe as the goal of the Christian: "In death there is no remembrance of thee: in the grave who shall give thee thanks?"

Therefore how audaciously false is the doctrine that the dead are alive, and either praising God in Heaven, or groaning in the Torments of Hell?

How long before men will cease to call such teachers as David liars, and concoct such frightful schemes to terrify the credulous, in order to accomplish their selfish purposes? How long must the realities of the Scriptures be supplanted by Damnable Heresies? Must Pagan Rome rule forever? Shall not the time come when the Protestant Church will see that this driving wheel of Popish machinery, (the Doctrine of Eternal Burning,) moves in direct opposition to God's word? Cannot they see, if they will, that to make this true, is to declare positively that Job, David, and Solomon are liars? Oh that they would consider how falsely they are accusing the Almighty, and return to the realities of the Scriptures!

So now, as this teaching to the effect that Death is Life, has been shown to be repugnant to all reason, loathsome to common sense, and positively contrary to the teachings of the Scriptures, we can proceed with the assurance that Life means Life, and that Death means Death. And with the light of the glorious Gospel of the Son of God shining upon our pathway, we can traverse the whole length before us, with but little to impede our progress.

EVERLASTING LIFE, AND EVERLASTING DEATH.

Says the Word: " God so loved the world, that he gave his only begotten Son " to die for us, "that whosoever believeth in him should not PERISH, but have EVER-LASTING LIFE." Here, Death is presented before us as the mighty ocean, into which, through their own sins, all had been immerged. Here we see that—not a few, but all —not one excepted, were or had been destined to Perish. " For all had sinned and come short of the glory of God." All were or had been in the mighty ocean of Death, and doomed to Perish.

God did not give His Son to save men from Temporal Death, or Perishing; for all thus perish. But He gave His Son to save them from Everlasting Perishing; and hence the saying, " That they might have everlasting life." There is no such a thing mentioned as that God gave His Son to die for us, that He might save us from an Everlasting Life,

4

in a Hell of Fire and Brimstone. No; but He gave His only begotten Son that we should not Perish, but have Everlasting Life; that we might be saved from that Everlasting Death to which all were destined. Hence, how plain is the fact that those who have not obtained Eternal Life, are still destined to the Everlasting Perishing, or Death?

Sin is the transgression of the law, and death is the penalty of sin. The First Death is the result of Adam's sin; but the Second, the Everlasting Death, if suffered, will be the result of our own sins. Therefore, when we are saved from the penalty of sin, we are saved from the Second, the Everlasting Death, which will be the Everlasting Punishment of the wicked. And how positively is this confirmed by the 24th verse of the Vth chapter of John, where Jesus says: "Verily, verily, I say unto you, He that heareth my word, and believeth on him that sent me, hath everlasting life, and shall not come into condemnation; but is passed FROM DEATH UNTO LIFE"?

Was it the Temporal Death from which they had been secured? No. It was the Everlasting Death.

Again, in 39th verse, He told the Jews to "search the Scriptures," for in them, said He, "ye think ye have eternal life;" but He gave them plainly to understand that unless they believed in Him, they had no life in them, but were a wreck on the broad ocean of universal Death. Then, in 40th verse, He said: "Ye will not come to me, that ye might have life." Then again, in Romans IId chapter and 6th verse, we read that "God will render to every man according to his deeds." And how is that? Why, "To them who by patient continuance in well doing seek for glory and honor and immortality, eternal life." So plainly and positively does every passage of Scripture that speaks of Eternal Life, teach us that it is the opposite of Everlasting Death, that the frivolity which is offered as evidence to prove that the wicked, after suffering the Second Death, shall live in a Hell of Fire and Brimstone, amounts to about as much as directing the mind to the stars at noonday, and trying to make it appear that they outshine the sun in his dazzling refulgence.

But to continue the consideration of the subject, we turn to the VIth chapter, 20th to 23d verses, and read: "For when ye were the servants of sin, ye were free from right-eousness. What fruit had ye then in those things whereof ye are now ashamed? for the end of those things is death. But now being made free from sin, and become servants to God, ye have your fruit unto holiness, and the end ever-lasting life. For the wages of sin is death; but the gift of God is eternal life through Jesus Christ our Lord."

Here, in the 21st verse, the Apostle asks the question: "What fruit had ye in those things whereof ye are now ashamed?" And then says he, "The end of those things is death." What death,—the termination of the natural life? Surely not, for that terminates with all. It would have been nonsense for the Apostle to have told them that the end of those things was Temporal Death; and if he had told them that the end of those things was an Everlasting Life,—the next verse would be an extract of nonsense. Therefore it was the Everlasting Death which he was speak-ing of, the only antidote for which, is, Eternal Life.

Now, in the face of all this, how foreign to common sense, and how belittling to the Scriptures, to say that the Second, or Everlasting Death, will be an Everlasting Life, an Eternal Burning in a Lake of Fire and Brimstone! It is exactly parallel with saying that the Eternal Life prom-ised the faithful, means Everlasting Death. And when we look at the attributes of God, and the horrid nature of the teaching referred to, the latter is found to be more con-sistent than the former.

But now turning to the Vth chapter of 1st John, 10th to 13th verse, again we see with what persistency the Eternal

Life is adhered to, and with what precision it is presented as the antidote for Everlasting Death. Says he: "He that believeth on the Son of God hath the witness in himself: he that believeth not God hath made him a liar, because he believeth not the record that God gave of his Son. And this is the record, that God hath given to us eternal life, and this life is in his Son. He that hath the Son, hath life; and he that hath not the Son of God, hath not life. These things have I written unto you that believe on the name of the Son of God; that ye may know that ye have eternal life, and that ye may believe on the name of the Son of God."

Here we have Eternal Life twice repeated, and thrice referred to. But is it expressed or referred to in such a manner as to convey the idea that it is something we cannot escape? Far from presenting such an idea! Such, however, is the teaching of those who have metamorphosed the truth, or rather, have, for it, substituted the herculean heresy of a Burning Hell between Death and the Resurrection, and the diabolical teaching. concerning the situation of the wicked thereafter. For they teach, that notwithstanding that the wicked, at the resurrection, (according to their doctrine,) will have been Burned in Hell for thousands of years, they shall, at the judgment, be tried, and then punished with —not Death, but an Everlasting Life in Flames of Indescribable Torment. But the Apostle, it seems, did not even imagine that humanity would even taint their lips with such a falsehood; but he limited the possession of Eternal Life, told who had it, and how it was to be obtained; and clearly showed that by obtaining it, they should escape from the mighty expanse of universal Death. For, said he: "This is the record, that God hath given us eternal life, and this life is in his Son;" and then said he, "He that hath the Son hath life; and he that hath not the Son of God hath not life." Then He gave them plainly to understand that to know that they had Eternal Life was enough for them to know, in order to complete their happiness; for that it was the reward of all their believing and doing. Therefore we see that if they had not obtained Eternal Life, they would have remained on the broad ocean of Everlasting Death; and that the Everlasting Life is salvation from Everlasting,—What! Life? How ridiculous! But how consistent to say, from Everlasting Death?

Now, turning to Philippians, IVth chapter, 3d verse, What do we see? Why, the Book of Life. Yes; and how does this phrase, Book of Life, ring out the death knell of this contrariety which makes Death Life, and Death and Life Eternal Life? Repeat the phrase, Book of Life. How indicative it is? How plainly it shows that the object in having such a book, is, that those whose names are written therein, are saved from Everlasting Death. And how plainly we can see what Paul thought of this Book of Life, when he said: "I entreat thee also true yoke fellow, help those women which labor with me in the gospel, with Clemet also, and with others of my fellow laborers, whose names are in the book of life." Why did he attach so much importance to their names being in the Book of Life? Why, because he knew that as their names were in the Book of Life, they had been numbered with those who were sure of escaping Everlasting Death; as shown in Revelation, IIId chapter and 5th verse: "He that overcometh, the same shall be clothed with white raiment; and I will not blot out his name out of the book of life, but I will confess his name before my Father, and before his angels."

Here we see the situation of the righteous; their names are in the Book of Life; and, at the time of reckoning, Jesus will confess their names before His Father, and before His angels; and then, being forever freed from the power of Death, they will enter into Life Eternal, and thus escape the Everlasting Death, which will be the Everlasting Punishment of the wicked.

Now, turning to Mark, Xth chapter, 17th verse, with a look at one great struggle for Eternal Life, I will relieve the reader from this part of the discourse.

Here we not only find men who are willing to accept Eternal Life, but, " when he was gone forth into the way," says Mark, " there came one running, and kneeled to him, and asked him, Good Master, what shall I do that I may inherit eternal life?" Yes, " inherit eternal life." But what does this prove? Why, it proves that he had become convinced that all men were or had been on the broad ocean of Everlasting Destruction; and that, unless he were rescued from it, nothing but Death was before him. It is equivalent to saying, Oh Lord, I am satisfied that outside of the redemption that is in Thee, all is Death. Therefore, Oh Lord, make me an object of Thy favor, and tell me how I may escape it! But what a ridiculous figure he would have presented if he had said, Oh Lord, I know that all shall live Eternally, but do tell me what I shall do that I may inherit Eternal Life!

Now, who could face the realities of God's word as they have been presented in the preceding, and not shrink from saying that Life, and not Death, is what we shall escape by inheriting Eternal Life? They may face the realities of fiendful imaginations, but they can never stand with such unholy teaching before the reality of the Divine Word. It is a sword of rebuke unto them, the opposite of all such fabrications.

But in order to hide from man the reality of his nature, the Apostatized Church taught, and it is still taught, that the spirit of man is, in itself, an entity. They tell us that man dies, and that his spirit is conveyed, either to heaven, or to hell; and that this spirit is, in reality, immortal man. They tell us that the spirit is the life, the reason, the soul, all the mental capacity, and, in fact, the whole being, except the fleshy shell with which it is clothed; and that, when death releases it from this, it is unclothed, immortal humanity; which, if it were visible, would be found to possess all the peculiarities of the person whose spirit it is. They teach that, as the larvated caterpillar perforates its cocoon and comes out a butterfly, just so, at death, man deserts his mortal shell and wings his way to the sunny region of immortal joys.

Now, no matter how much this teaching is disguised, this is the reality of the case; and is, in substance, the doctrine of the heathen philosophers to the effect that death is but the dropping of the cumbersome part of man's immortal self, that rustic shell which excludes him from the liberty which his immortal self is fitted for, independently of the resurrection, he being of just such a nature, that Death, instead of being a reality of punishment, is the gateway to Eternal Felicity.*

This is the doctrine of those who scout the teaching of Job, when he says: "Man lieth down, and riseth not: till the heavens be no more, they shall not awake, nor be raised out of their sleep." Hence, instead of accepting God's word, they tell us that man is not as the flood that decayeth and drieth up, but that he is as the tree, which, though cut down, will shoot forth as a plant. And thus the realities of the Scriptures are spurned from them, and the productions of apostasy are presented in their stead.

Again, while condemning the teachings of Job, by maintaining the doctrines of the heathen, they do not escape telling us that Paul is a liar,—that there is no truth in what he has taught concerning the future state,—that his ideas of the resurrection are erroneous,—that we cannot rely upon what he has said in reference to the resurrection of Jesus; and that he is not to be believed when he says that in the absence of the resurrection, those who have fallen asleep in Christ have perished. Yea, when he tells them that Death

---

* For proof of this the reader is referred to the teachings of Plato, Socrates, Cicero, or, to those of any other heathen writer who has treated the subject of futurity.

is a reality, they spurn it from them, and by teaching that Death is the gateway to a glorious future, they make void his declarations, and might as well say that what Festus told him is true; that his teaching to the effect that the dead are not alive in heaven, but that they are in their graves, and that there shall be a resurrection of the dead, is the wild imagination of a madman, instead of "the words of truth and soberness."

LIFE, AN EXISTENCE: DEATH, A NON-EXISTENCE.

But that we may more clearly see that, as Life constitutes an existence, so Death constitutes a non-existence, we turn to the VIth chapter of Romans, and read: "For when ye were the servants of sin, ye were free from righteousness. What fruit had ye then in those things whereof ye are now ashamed? for the end of those things is death. But now being made free from sin, and become servants to God, ye have your fruit unto holiness, and the end everlasting life. For the wages of sin is death; but the gift of God is eternal life through Jesus Christ our Lord."

Now, how conspicuously is the discrimination between Life and Death presented before us? (But what a shame that common sense must be brought down to such a level as to make it necessary to prove that Death does not mean Life!) How emphatically does the Apostle prove that Death is that which Life is not, when he says: "For when ye were the servants of sin, ye were free from righteousness. What fruit had ye in those things whereof ye are now ashamed? for the end of those things is death. But now being made free from sin, and become servants to God, ye have your fruit unto holiness, and the end everlasting life. For the wages of sin is death; but the gift of God is eternal life through Jesus Christ our Lord"? He shows us that when they were the servants of sin, they were free from, or had nothing to do with righteousness. Hence the difference between righteousness and sin, for Paul shows us that sin is that which righteousness is not. But why not sin be righteousness as much as Death is Life? Verily, it is. But he continues and says, The end of those things is,—What! Life? Oh no! But why not? Would not a Life in a Blazing Hell be as much a reality of Life as a Life in Heaven? Certainly it would! And, if it were possible for such a state of things to exist, those who experience Life in felicity would be a thousand times behind in desiring the continuance of that Life, when compared with the desire of the others to have theirs end. But while presenting before them the reality of their condition whilst in a state of sin, Paul told them that "the end of those things was death;"* and then said he, "But now being made free from sin, and become servants to God, ye have your fruit unto holiness, and the end everlasting life." But why should he not have said Death? for if Death in such constructions as the preceding, could mean Life, (not that it could mean Life in any others,) Life could just as certainly mean Death; for they were in sin, and the end of sin was Death. Therefore, to say that the Death spoken of meant Life, would be just as absurd as to say that the Life spoken of meant Death.

Again, the dust to which Adam returned, was no more Adam after he had returned to it, than it, the same dust, had been Adam before he was made of it; and the breath of life was no more Adam after it had returned to God Who gave it, than it had been Adam before He breathed it into him. Hence the absurdity of either the dust or the spirit being the man.

---

*The reader should be careful to discriminate between the First Death, and the Second Death; for, as is almost useless to say, had they been ever so righteous they would have suffered the First Death. The end of such things, therefore, will be the Second, or Everlasting Death; and the end of obedience to God will be the Second, or Everlasting Life.

God made man of the dust of the ground, and thus made, though devoid of all animation, he was man complete. Then God breathed into his nostrils the breath of life, by which he became a living soul; and therefore, a soul is exactly what he was: He was no more than a soul, and there is not—there cannot be—either here or hereafter, a soul that is anything less.

THE SPIRIT IS NOT THE MAN NOR THE SOUL, BUT THE ANIMATING POWER BY WHICH THE ONE BECOMES THE OTHER. Therefore, when the breath of life goes forth and returns to God Who gave it,* the man returns to his dust, and the soul is not in existence. But the natural death, or termination of the natural life, is but temporal; and this death is experienced by all, and is the exact opposite of the life. The life is what we live, and the death terminates it; that is, first we live, and then we do not live. Hence, as the first, or temporal death is the opposite of the first, or temporal life, so the Second Death will be the opposite of the Second, or Eternal Life. Therefore, to assert that the Second Death will be an Eternal Life, would be just as conspicuously false, as to say that the Second, or Eternal Life will be an Everlasting Death. There would not be a shadow of difference between the two assertions. But Life means Life, and Death means Death. As one constitutes an existence, so the other constitutes a nonexistence. As the saint will be rewarded with the Second, or Eternal Life, so the sinner will be punished with the Second, or Everlasting Death; for, as the Psalmist has declared, " The wicked shall perish, and the enemies of the

---

* Very important to understand. here, is the fact that it is not necessary for the spirit, or breath of life to go to heaven, in order to return to God; for God is everywhere. The spirit is what God breathed into man; and therefore, when it returns, it goes back, just what it came; not something that has become corrupt, but animation; that which did not constitute any part of man, but what made animate the man, after he had been made.

It is not the animation or breath of life that fails, but the organism when worn out, will no longer run: and thus the animation is—not destroyed, but forced out; and thus out. has—but not as the superlative of humanity, or a sinful, sunken, miserable wretch who came from the nostrils of the Almighty, returned to God Who gave it. And as the spirit is the animating power, and only such, the reason why a man lives, is because he is animated, and the reason why a man is dead, is because he is not animated.

Lord shall be as the fat of lambs: they shall consume; into smoke shall they consume away."

That the wicked shall consume into smoke, in the lake of fire, and that the above-mentioned passage refers to that event, is both plain and positive. For, at the consummation, there will be but one generation of the wicked together; and the destroying of them temporally will not fulfill the above-mentioned destruction. But, in the 38th verse of this, the XXXVIIth Psalm, David tells us when it shall be fulfilled; for says he: " The transgressors shall be destroyed together: the end of the wicked shall be cut off." Therefore, the time when the wicked "shall be cut off," will be, when, in the lake of fire, "the transgressors shall be destroyed together;" and when, after the last resurrection, they will be together for the first time.

Adam was punished with temporal death, and therefore, at the resurrection he will live again; for that event will terminate the time that he is to remain dead. But those who refuse salvation through Christ, will be punished—not for Adam's, but for their own sins, with Everlasting Death; that is, the one has been consigned to the First Death, to not live again, for a time; the others, as has been decreed, shall die the Second Death, and not live again at all.

These are the simple realities of the Scriptures concerning the present and the intermediate states; and the plain teaching concerning the reward of the righteous, which is Eternal Life, and the punishment of the wicked, which will be Everlasting Death.

But after the Church had apostatized and become corrupt to such an extent that selfish greed and tyranny prevailed, and their consciences had become as seared with a hot iron, in order to carry out their tyranny and establish the supreme dominion of the Apostatized Church by bringing the necks of the Laity under the iron heel of the Clergy, they added to their already accumulated stock of heathenish dogmas, the damnable heresy of an Eternal Burning in a Hell of Fire and Brimstone, where they would enter at death, and be punished thenceforth and forever; by means of which, and the heresy of the Wafer, or handling God with their hands, they made the Laity subjects of their extortions all the days of their lives, and shared much of their fortunes at death.

But how this doctrine of Eternal Burning has continued, how it exists so generally, is truly mysterious! How men can lift their eyes towards heaven and declare that God has appointed as a punishment for the erring of our race, a Lake of Fire and Brimstone; in which they shall Burn Eternally in order to Gratify His Vengeance, without ever being able to Satisfy it, is strange indeed! and aside from willful perversion, cannot be accounted for, except that, as was the case with Luther and the Wafer, instead of being an impression of the usual cast, it has been so powerfully forced upon man from youth to old age, through many generations, that it has become an indentation of the mind that nothing can smooth; so that everything that crosses it must bend to this unnatural curvity.

Yet it is, nevertheless, an abominable heresy, and more foreign to the attributes of the Almighty, than is the tiny switch of a tender mother, to the ruthless club of a midnight assassin. But not only do the Scriptures condemn the doctrine of Eternal Torment, but those who teach it, prove by their actions in their dealings with one another, that such cruelty, instead of belonging to God, is foreign, even to man. For were a woman to commit a crime against her husband, and he punish her by holding her hand in the fire until the flesh burned off the bones, he would be pronounced one of the most cruel beings in the world; and if he were to escape justice, he would be hunted as a wild beast; and when brought to trial and condemned, he would be pronounced worthy of thrice the punishment that the law could inflict. And he would have been tried and condemned by men, most of whom, perhaps, believed that God would take that same woman, for that same crime that she had committed against her husband, and put—not only her hand, but her whole self into a Lake of Fire and Brimstone;—not for half an hour—not for a day—not for a year—nor for ten thousand years only, but for all Eternity. Also that this Burning of her in a Blazing Hell would be so agreeable to the determination of the Almighty that no pity could be excited, no mercy shown; but that, there, in that Lake of Fire she should gnash, and groan, and wail Eternally. Oh! how horrid the picture! And what a terrible crime, even in the light of their own actions, to charge God with such cruelty!

A LOOK AT THE CHARACTER OF GOD.

But now let us look at the character of God—not as blackened with the smut of Eternal Burning, but as He has revealed Himself unto us.

The most severe of all the attributes of God, is Justice; and this Justice was manifested at the beginning, when, after man, as a free agent, had been placed in the garden, and it was said unto him: "Of every tree of the garden thou mayst freely eat: But of the tree of the knowledge of good and evil, thou shalt not eat of it: for in the day that thou eatest thereof thou shalt surely die."

We here see, that, had man obeyed, he would have lived. But he disobeyed, and the sentence of Death was pronounced upon him, thus: "Because thou hast hearkened unto the voice of thy wife, and hast eaten of the tree, of which I commanded thee, saying, Thou shalt not eat of it: cursed is the ground for thy sake; in sorrow shalt thou eat

of it all the days of thy life; Thorns also and thistles shall
it bring forth to thee; and thou shalt eat the herb of the
field. In the sweat of thy face shalt thou eat bread, till
thou return unto the ground; for out of it wast thou taken:
for dust thou art, and unto dust shalt thou return."

"Dust thou art, and unto dust shalt thou return." This
dissolution, this returning to what he had been made of,
this, and this only, is death; and this is the severest punishment that God has ever yet inflicted, or ever will inflict
upon man.

Now, to the Advocates of Eternal Torment, I would say:
Why did not God tell Adam that in the day in the which
he ate of the forbidden fruit he should be consigned to an
Eternal Life, in the Flames of a Literal Hell? Did He
want to deceive Adam? Can you account for your doctrine? You may, through the lower channels of heathenism, but not in God's word; it all testifies against you.
Yea, instead of giving you an inch of ground to stand
upon, it sweeps you from its face, and places your doctrine
among the damnable heresies which the Apostle foresaw
would be brought into the Church; and plainly shows that
of all that are damnable, it is about the chief.

Having now seen the extreme of God's severity, in Rigid
Justice, let me ask: Has man nothing to look to God for
but Justice? What does the Apostle say? Why, "looking
for the mercy of God unto eternal life." What a modification! Not looking for mercy only, but "for the mercy of
God unto eternal life."

But let us go to the beginning, and see what is the first
thing presented to our minds as transpiring in relation to
man. Is it a manifestation of the work of Torment? No;
but of Love, the Love that God bore towards man before
he was in existence, and which "is manifested," as the
Apostle says, "in these last times." Yea, even the manifestation of His Love in that "he gave his only begotten

Son, that whosoever believeth in him should not perish, but have everlasting life."

Now, what is shown of the attributes of God by this? Does it not manifest the existence of Love towards us that cannot be equalled, and that before we were in existence? It is manifest that God had such great Love towards us that He made wonderful provision for us; even such, that, if man should, as a free agent, choose evil rather than good, He would suffer His only begotten Son to die, that after man had sinned against Him, he might escape Everlasting Death, through this wonderful provision; which, it is evident, could have been the production of nothing but the superlation of Love.

Here we see unparalleled Love in God the Father, in that before we were in existence, He made provision for us by the foreordaining of His beloved Son. "And when the fullness of the time was come," or when the full time had come, "*while we were yet sinners*, God gave His Son to die for us, that we might not Perish, but have Everlasting Life;" that, although we had become estranged from Him through the disobedience of Adam, and our own sins, through sanctification of the Spirit and the sprinkling of the blood of Jesus Christ, He might make possible our obedience; and, by accepting this obedience, brought about through Christ, as a substitute for that which He had required of Adam, bring about our salvation. What Love! Who can express it! Language cannot tell how He loved us! Nothing but a full view of ourselves, a look to Gethsemane, and thence to Calvary, can make us understand it.

Yet, although God the Father had all this Love for us before we were in existence, and has manifested it unto us, the Advocates of Eternal Burning declare that He possesses that Insatiable Vengeance which the most terrible torment that the mind is capable of conceiving, cannot satisfy. And then they claim that by thus teaching, instead of sinning against Him, they glorify Him.

This, though damnable, it seems that, in many, is blind heresy.

But not only has the Father done all that is presented in the foregoing, but, without respect of person, He reaches forth in the Unlimited Capacity of Himself, and speaks to all; urges them to repentance, presses the necessity of faith in the Atonement, and thus draws them to the Mighty Succorer, whose arms are ever open to receive them.

THE MIGHTY SUCCORER.

Now, as this Mighty Succorer is the Son of Mary, let us pause awhile, that we may see God as revealed in Jesus Christ. For, having been forever freed from the power of death, with all power conferred upon Him, He is the Mighty God to Whom His Father, Jehovah, has committed all judgment. "For the Father judgeth no man, but hath committed all judgment unto the Son;" and therefore the Son is Judge. And in this Judge we have—not only Omniscience, but Human Sympathy therewith combined; for God "hath appointed a day in the which he will judge the world in righteousness by that MAN whom he hath ordained."

Now, what kind of a character did He manifest during His natural life? Did He manifest hatred towards mankind? Did He curse Jerusalem? No; but He wept over it. And again, while yielding His life upon the cross, referring to His murderers, He said: "Father, forgive them; for they know not what they do!"

And is this the one who will consign the erring of humanity to Eternal Burning in the Flames of a Literal Hell? Were they to say, He will remove even the pangs of the Second Death, they would have the better side of the question.

65

But, though God can be just, "and the Justifier of them that believe in Jesus," He cannot be just, "and the Justifier of them " that reject His Unspeakable Gift, and refuse to believe on Him that they may have Eternal Life. Therefore they must reap the reward of their doings, and suffer the punishment of Everlasting Death.

Again, Jesus says: "Therefore doth my Father love me, because I lay down my life for the sheep." What did He lay down His life for? Why, He laid down His life for the sheep. And who were the sheep? Why sinners were the sheep. Hence we see that "while we were yet sinners, Christ died for the ungodly." He did not die for a single act of righteousness of any man's, but He died for sinners.

God loved sinners before Christ died, and still loves sinners; and Jesus, Who bled and died for sinners, now sits at the right hand of God the Father, Who always loved sinners, to plead with the Father for sinners. Therefore we see that the work of God the Father, the Son, and the Holy Ghost, is all love, and that to sinners.

Yet, aside from mercy and love, the case of the sinner will be parallel with that of Adam's.* Adam failed to obey, and God punished him with that which He had warned him that He would inflict, and that was Death; which is just what He has warned the descendants of Adam that He will inflict upon them, if they do not obey Him in the Gospel of His Son Jesus Christ; the only difference being (except as regards duration) that which any one can understand who can count two, or knows the difference between first and second; for the one is the First Death, and the other will be the Second Death.

Now, as all that God has manifested towards us in the work of redemption is Love, how clearly it is to be seen that the least punishment by which the wicked can be made an

*Though Mercy and Love, both preceded and followed his fall, Adam, in the Garden was dealt with in accordance with Rigid Justice.

5

example and forever removed from the righteous, is that which God will use; yea, is that which He has chosen. And manifest it is, that that least will be the Second Death!

But those who sneer at the idea that Death is Death, even in the face of all the Love that God has manifested towards sinners—in the face of the fact that the Son of God, willingly and of Himself, laid down His life for sinners, turn and tell us that the destruction of the wicked would be but a shadow of punishment in the sight of the Almighty. They tell us that ten thousand Deaths would be but as a beginning of their punishment; and that nothing can gratify the Vengeance of Jehovah but the Eternal groanings of the wicked in Flames of Literal Fire. Therefore they teach that incomparable punishment, compared with which the punishment that God will inflict, is as the dust of the balance, or the slight glimmering of a shadow. Yea, the horrid torment, the unceasing misery which they tell us that God has in store for erring humanity,* is that which the wildest imagination, the most hyperbolical capacity with all its powers concentrated, could not possibly magnify; and this they present before us as that which, and which only, can gratify the Vengeance of the Almighty; and, say they, even that can never satisfy it. Oh that they would see their sin! And now I repeat, Thanks be to God that such teaching is not mine!

Again, how does the doctrine of Eternal Burning affect the character of Jesus when we regard Him as what, in reality, He is, our brother—a real—a natural brother,—flesh, as our flesh—bone, as our bone; and when we view Him as our Great High Priest, who can be touched with a feeling of our infirmities; and when we remember that He is the Organism of Sympathy between God and man? It takes from His glory. It is a reproach unto Him;—His teachings prove it such.

---

*This, however, according to their doctrine, was commenced nearly six thousand years ago.

Who cannot see that if Jesus should consign the erring of our race to Eternal Burning in a Hell of Literal Fire and Brimstone, He would, by that act, cause ten thousand times more misery than all that He would have accomplished in behalf of humanity could possibly amount to? The misery would outbalance, ten million times, all that the righteous could possibly enjoy!

No wonder that there are so many skeptics! No wonder that so many of the higher order of intellects, have, through this direful dogma, rejected the Scriptures, and spurned such teachings from them as unbefitting well-balanced minds!

And still again, How does this monstrosity appear when we look at ourselves, and say: Could we do this, could we consign our brethren to the Flames of an Eternal Hell? We might look at the destruction of the wicked, and say, It is but justice; and then we would cease. Hence, then, how terrible to charge Jesus with being capable of consigning His Adamic brethren to the Flames of an Eternal Hell!

But why dwell longer upon this? Why should all the facts of Scripture be gathered to disprove such an unreasonable, unholy doctrine;—a doctrine that charges a God of Justice, a God of Mercy, yea, even a God of Love with possessing that Insatiable Vengeance which nothing but the groanings of the victims of a Blazing Hell can gratify? Again, I say, why dwell upon this? What have they to support such an idea? What is the basis of this unholy doctrine? It is based upon the positive falsehood that Death means Life. It was founded upon the destruction of truth; it was reared upon the ruins of Scripture.

It says to the "holy men of God" who "spake as they were moved by the Holy Ghost," Your teachings are false, you have taught us lies. It says to the Inspired Preacher, You tell us that the dead know not anything, whereas they know all that they knew in this life, and thrice as much more. And you, David, tell us that "the dead praise not the Lord," whereas they are always before Him in heaven, and praise Him continually. You say that, in death, there is no remembrance of God; whereas the dead do not only remember the Lord, but they are the guardian angels of their living friends, and always have them in remembrance. You ask, Who, from the grave, shall praise the Lord? and so you show that you know nothing about the dead; for the dead are alive in heaven, praising God amidst the greatest felicity, or in Hell, suffering the Torment of Burning Flames. You tell us that man's breath goeth forth, that he returneth to his earth, and that, in that very day, his thoughts perish. You might as well tell us that that is the last of him until the resurrection, for you try to make us believe that there will be a resurrection. What nonsense! Who taught you this! It is nothing strange that one who knows so little as you do, should believe that "the dead know not anything;" it is not the dead, but such as you, who know nothing.

This is what this monstrosity, this fiendish production of unscrupulous apostates is founded upon; and though angels from heaven were to declare it truth, it could not be other than falsehood.

THE SAME STORY.

Now, passing from David to Job, we have but a continuation of the same story; for, says Job, XIVth chapter and 7th verse: " There is hope of a tree, if it be cut down, that it will sprout again, and that the tender branch thereof will not cease. Though the root thereof wax old in the earth, and the stalk thereof die in the ground; Yet through the scent of water it will bud, and bring forth boughs like a plant."

Here, Job says "there is hope of a tree, if it be cut down;" and then says he, "Man dieth and wasteth away: yea, man giveth up the ghost, and where is he?" In Heaven, or in Hell, say the Advocates of Eternal Burning. But Job continues, and might as well say they are liars; and if they had preceded him, it is evident that he would have done so; for he says: "As the waters fail from the sea, and the flood decayeth and drieth up; So man lieth down, and riseth not: till the heavens be no more, they shall not awake, nor be raised out of their sleep."

Now, in this we also see that when they close their eyes in Death, this Death is their sleep. But what absurdity this would be if the doctrine of Eternal Burning were true! Could they sleep in the Flames of Hell? Or, could they be awakened out of a sleep of thousands of years, whilst during that period they had been enjoying the fullness of their reward in heaven? O how preposterous the idea that Death is not Death, but Life! How belittling to common sense, and how foreign to the least shadow of truth, is this teaching that when a man Dies he does not Die, but is simply stripped of just enough of his composition to develop the full reality of his immortal self; and that thus freed from his rustic tenement, he wings his way to the Realm of Glory, or, if of the other class, is nevertheless immortal, and is driven to the Flames of Hell; when all this is because Death is not Death, but Life; because Everlasting Destruction means Everlasting Living, where they will not be destroyed at all; and because, when the end of the wicked shall be cut off, that will be when they will begin to wish that they had never had a beginning such as never could be cut off.

But who does not know that when flood is decayed and dried up, that it is gone, that it does not exist? And who dare say that Job does not teach that this is the case with the man? For he says: "Man dieth, and wasteth away: yea, man giveth up the ghost, and where is he?" Then he tells us that, "as the waters fail from the sea, and the flood decayeth and drieth up; So man lieth down, and riseth not;" and that, "till the heavens be no more, they shall not awake, nor be raised out of their sleep."

This amounts to more, (in favor of the sentiments of this book,) a thousand times, than all that the Advocates of Eternal Burning can produce in favor of their worse than heathenish story of a Burning Hell between Death and the Resurrection.

But still Job continues, and says: "O that thou wouldst keep me secret, until thy wrath be past, that thou wouldst appoint me a set time, and remember me!" And so he tells us what he knows about Death, and then he asks the question: "If a man die, shall he live again?" Then, as if receiving an answer to the effect that he should, he says: "All the days of my appointed time will I wait, till my change come. Thou shalt call, and I will answer thee, thou wilt have a desire to the work of thine hands."

Thus we are told, and plainly too, that Job asked God the question: "If a man die, shall he live again?" and that God told him that he should, and that it should be at an appointed time; that then Job desired that God would hide him in the grave, and there keep him secret until His wrath was past; and that, having received the promise that he should not be left there, but that he should come forth at the set time, he expressed his confidence in God by saying, "Thou shalt call, and I will answer thee;" for I know that Thou carest for me, for I am the work of Thy hands.

But the brazen-faced falsifiers of the Scriptures, in order to have Job in heaven, make it appear that he was acting a part, little better than that of a buffoon.

Yet Job continues, and as it were, standing in the presence of the Almighty, he sets his seal to what he has said; and, in so doing, shows us that the teachings of those who say that Death is not a reality, are as false as the fables of the heathen. Says he : " The waters were the stones : thou washest away the things which grow out of the dust of the earth; and thou destroyest the hope of man. Thou prevailest for ever against him, and he passeth; thou changest his countenance, and sendest him away. His sons come to honor, and *he knoweth it not;* and they are brought low, *but he perceiveth it not of them.*"

Emphatically is this to the effect that the case with the man is just as Solomon has since declared it to be; that is, that " THE DEAD KNOW NOT ANY THING;" and also, that their rest is together, in the dust.

Not once does Job mention such a thing, or even intimate such a thing as soaring to the region of glory. But heart-stricken, steeped in sorrow, and death staring him in the face, he looks at the grave, and then to heaven, and says : "If a man die, shall he live again?" Then, when the answer comes that God will remember him, that he shall come forth at the resurrection, he says : "All the days of my appointed time will I wait, till my change come : Thou shalt call, and I will answer thee : thou wilt have a desire to the work of thine hands." And again, " Though after my skin worms destroy this body, yet in my flesh shall I see God : Whom I shall see for myself, and mine eyes shall behold, and not another; though my reins be consumed within me."

So we see that it was Job who lived, Job who died, Job who was laid in the grave, and Job who was to wait there until the set time. And we see that when he shall have come forth, it will be the same Job that had lain in the grave, or rested in the dust, from the time of his death, until the set time, the morning of the resurrection.

Not once did Job speak of the joys of heaven as before him, between Death and the Resurrection. Not once did the Fiction of the Fiery Kingdom reach the outermost bound of his imagination. The grave only was his hiding-place. The remembering of him by the Almighty was his comfort, and the assurance that he should be called forth in the morning of the resurrection, was his hope.

Here, again we see how foreign to the teachings of the "holy men of God who spake as they were moved by the Holy Ghost," is this doctrine that, at death, the righteous go to the Realm of Glory, and the wicked to the Flames of Hell. Destitute of a shadow of foundation do these truths leave this worse than heathenish fabrication? Positively and clearly do they show, that between death and the resurrection, MAN KNOWS NOTHING. And clearly this proves that the Second Death, instead of being what the Advocates of Eternal Burning would have it, an Eternal Life, is an Everlasting Death.

If men, after the first death, were never to be resurrected, the first death would be Everlasting, and they would never live again. But there will be a resurrection, and therefore the first death is temporal. But after the wicked shall have been cast into the lake of fire, where "the transgressors shall be destroyed together," which will be the Second Death, there will be no more resurrection; and therefore it follows that the Second, will be an Everlasting Death, which, and which only, will be the Everlasting Punishment of the wicked. Therefore we see that the difference between the punishment which God has determined as the portion of the wicked, and that of an Eternal Burning in a Blazing Hell, is as the difference between the least that is possible, and the greatest that the wildest, the most hyperbolical capacity could possibly conceive of. And manifest, therefore, it is, that this doctrine of Eternal Burning should be rejected —not as only unreasonable and false, but as what, in reality, it is, a disgrace to the name of Christianity, and a Scandal against the Almighty.

THE JUDGMENT SCENE.

Now, turning to Matthew XXVth chapter, we find thirty-three verses occupied with the subject of reward and punishment. But what do they teach? What becomes of the fiend-like story of the Fiery Kingdom, where the wicked, by the Advocates of Eternal Burning, are sent, at death, and punished in Flaming Fire?

You shall see. " When the Son of man shall come in his glory, and all the holy angels with him, then shall he sit upon the throne of his glory: And before him shall be gathered all nations: and he shall separate them one from another, as a shepherd divideth his sheep from the goats." When shall this be? Why, when "he shall come in his glory, and all the holy angels with him"—not when the righteous go to glory, and to the holy angels.

"And he shall set the sheep on his right hand, but the goats on the left. Then shall the King say unto them on his right hand, Come, ye blessed of my Father, inherit the kingdom prepared for you from the foundation of the world." And then He tells them why, for what reasons they shall be thus rewarded; for He says, " I was a hungered and ye gave me meat: I was thirsty, and ye gave me drink: I was a stranger, and ye took me in : Naked, and ye clothed me : I was sick, and ye visited me : I was in prison, and ye came unto me."

But do we hear the righteous say, Yes, Lord, we did so, and wish that we had done more; for we have been richly rewarded by the enjoyment of heaven for thousands of years, and we bless the day, when, through the gate of death, we escaped from the sorrowful scenes of earth, to the felicitous region of Eternal Glory? Is this their answer? No. This is the story of the Fabulists. But now let us have theirs.

"Then shall the righteous answer him, saying, Lord, when saw we thee a hungered, and fed thee? or thirsty, and gave thee drink? When saw we thee a stranger, and took thee in? or naked, and clothed thee? Or when saw we thee sick, or in prison, and came unto thee?" Does this look like having been enjoying the reward of their doings for centuries? What surprise they manifest at the solution of the matter? But not a word do we hear from them concerning the intermediate state.

So, when Christ shall have come in His glory, and all the holy angels with Him, and shall have sat upon the throne of His glory, and shall have had all nations before Him, and they shall have been separated, and everything settled, then, for the above-mentioned reasons, the righteous shall enter upon their reward—not as the shadows of what they had been, but as resurrected and glorified humanity.

Then the wicked will begin to inquire why they are to be punished. Poor creatures! Tormented for thousands of years in a Blazing Hell, and will have just found out that they are to be punished! But passing this for the present, we see that the wicked shall be punished for the opposite of that for which the righteous shall be rewarded, and that both reward and punishment will not precede, but follow the coming of Christ in His glory, accompanied by His holy angels.

But how foreign to all this is the doctrine that, at Death, the righteous pass to the Realm of Glory, and the wicked to the Flames of Hell? If those wicked ones had been Burned in Hell for centuries, Why did they not say something about it? Why did they not so much as say, Lord, we have been Burned in Hell for five hundred years, will not that suffice? Surely, if they had been, some a thousand, and some six thousand years suffering the Torment of Burning Flames, they would at least have ventured to mention it before a righteous judge, as a reason why they should not have been punished longer!

THE RESURRECTED.

But now we will pass from visions of the future, to scenes that have been witnessed upon earth.

Where are the stories of those who have been raised from the dead? What did the Child tell Elijah concerning the sunny region where he flapped his angel wings and soared around and through the heavenly throng and feasted his infant vision with beholding the unspeakable glory of the abode of the ransomed? Did he say, Oh Elijah! you have blessed my mother, but you have cursed me; for you have torn me from the bosom of angels and again brought me into this sorrowful world? Was this his story? No. He died, and then was brought to life again; and when this is said, his story is fully told.

But let us go on. Where did the Widow's Son say he had been? Where are the beauties of the heavenly region as pictured by him when Christ raised him from the dead? Did he frown upon the world and say, O that I were with them again that I might again partake of the joys of immortality in that heavenly region whence I came? Poor creatures who have such a faith to sustain! they could do much better with Socrates or Plato, than they can with the Bible.

Again, how is it that we hear nothing concerning this matter from the Chief, as it were, of the resurrected, the beloved Lazarus? Was he not a spectacle to the whole Jewish nation? Were not the eyes of all directed towards him? How is it, then, that we do not hear from him upon this subject? Why did he not tell those skeptical Jews that whilst his body was lying in the grave, his soul, or all that he had been, except the fleshy shell that he left behind, was felicitating in the realm of glory, amidst the angelic host and those who had gone before him? Why did he not thus present Death before them as the beginning of a glorious Life, as do the Advocates of Eternal Burning, who never had an opportunity of viewing the other side of the grave, as they call it; for he had been dead, and raised from the dead, and was then before them? But no, not one word do we hear from him, of either Heaven, or of Hell! It was Lazarus who had been raised from the dead. It was the one to whose grave the mourners had followed Jesus, and it was thence, they knew He had brought him. They knew of nothing else, they thought of nothing else. It was not the one who had been brought down from heaven, but the one who had been brought forth from the grave; the one who had been dead and knew nothing for four days, and of course told them nothing, because he had nothing to tell. And those who were present, being ignorant of the fabulous stories of the ages of apostasy, or acquainted with such teachings, only as heathenism, did not so much as ask him a single question concerning the glories of Heaven, or the existence of a Burning Hell.

Now, where would have been Christ's glory in raising Lazarus from the dead, if the present day teaching had been His? Why should He have wanted to make those loved ones miserable by bringing their brother from the glories of heaven to re-occupy that decaying shell and again dwell amidst the sorrows of earth? Why did He not say to those weeping ones, Dry up your tears, your brother is in heaven; the shell which you have laid in the grave is as nothing; it would be cruelty for you to have him brought back, or for Me to call him from that holy, happy place? But was this His comforting? No. Yet it is evident that if such comfort had been in existence, they would have received it; for He loved Lazarus and those who mourned over him, His sympathy united with the sympathy of those weeping ones, and He wept; yea, even groaned within Himself. But He did not weep because Lazarus was in the vigor of immortal bloom, amidst the glories of heaven, but because he was dead and in the grave; and therefore His comforting was, " Thy brother shall rise again."

And how plainly does the fact that there was not a single question asked concerning the whereabout of the soul of Lazarus during the time he had been dead, show that those Jews and Christians did not believe the heathenish stories about the souls, or spirits of men being—some in heaven, and some in hell?

It is evident beyond dispute, that, if such a belief had existed, the most prominent feature of that gathering together unto Lazarus would have been the inquiries concerning his journey to the celestial clime, and the glorious realities of that holy, happy place.

How plainly does every truth display the falsity of the doctrine concerning the righteous being in heaven, and the wicked being in hell, between Death and the Resurrection! And how plainly do these truths stand out in bold condemnation of the idea of an Eternal Burning of the erring of humanity in Flames of Fire and Brimstone? For as certainly as the First Death terminates the First Life, which fact, (that it does,) is so clearly shown by the cases of the resurrected referred to, just as certainly will the Second Death terminate the Second Life!

A SKETCH OF THE TESTIMONY OF PAUL.

But, again let us see how the doctrine of Eternal Burning corresponds with the teaching of the great Apostle of the Gentiles.

In 1st Corinthians, XVth chapter, commencing at 12th verse, we read: "Now if Christ be preached that rose from the dead, how say some among you that there is no resurrection of the dead? But if there be no resurrection of the dead, then is not Christ risen: And if Christ be not risen, then is our preaching vain, and your faith is also vain. Yea, and we are found false witnesses of God; because we have testified of God that he raised up Christ: whom he raised not up, if so be that the dead rise not. For if the dead rise not, then is not Christ raised. And if Christ be not raised, your faith is vain; ye are yet in your sins. *Then they also which are fallen asleep in Christ are perished.*"

Mark it, reader, it was not the wicked only, but the righteous also, who, in the absence of the resurrection, had perished! for Paul says: "If Christ be not raised, ... they also which are fallen asleep in Christ are perished."

Now, if they had gone to heaven, at death, this assertion of Paul's to the effect that in the absence of the resurrection, those who had fallen asleep in Christ had perished, would be a positive falsehood. Therefore we clearly see that the place for this doctrine of the immortality of man aside from the resurrection, is with the heresies, which, by designing apostates have been brought into the Church; and that, just as in the absence of the resurrection, those who had died, would remain dead forever,* just so those who shall be punished with the Second Death, from which there will be no resurrection, will ever remain dead; and that, thus dead, never to be resurrected, they will have been punished with Everlasting Death, their Everlasting Punishment.

A SKETCH OF THE TESTIMONY OF PETER.

So now, having seen the teaching of the great Apostle of the Gentiles, let us see what is said in reference to this question, by the great Apostle of the Jews.

Now, how disgraceful to the name of Christianity does this doctrine concerning the punishing of the wicked in a

---

* It should not be supposed that the phrase, For ever, because the time implied by it, was limited according to the nature of the case in which it was employed, (in Bible times,) could not have been used in reference to the Deity, and things regarded as Eternal. For whilst it was said of God, Who is Eternal and Omnipotent, "Him that liveth for ever and ever," it was also said, "He is a great God." Hence, For ever, did not mean Eternally, any more than Great meant Omnipotent.

Flaming Hell for thousands of years prior to the Resurrection and Judgment, appear, when we look at the plain truth as he has presented it before us! For, says this Oracle of God, 2d Peter, IId chapter, and 9th verse: "The Lord knoweth how to deliver the godly out of temptations, and to reserve the unjust unto the day of judgment to be punished."

If, now, it be admitted that this writing is the result of Inspiration, or even of what Peter saw and heard while with Christ, without direct Inspiration, this, the 9th verse, should put to the blush, and silence forever, those who try to make it appear that prior to the Resurrection and Judgment, the wicked are suffering the Torment of Burning Flames. Here they come face to face with Peter, and must condemn him as being guilty of falsehood, or be condemned as being positively guilty of such, by him.

But now let us closely compare the teachings of those who tell us that, at death, the righteous go to heaven, and that the unjust are sent to hell to be punished in Burning Flames, with the language of the Apostle as recorded in the above-quoted verse.

The Apostle tells us that "THE UNJUST ARE RESERVED UNTO THE DAY OF JUDGMENT TO BE PUNISHED;" and therefore shows an interval of thousands of years between the death of many of the unjust, and the time that they shall be punished; and that there is none of the dead who have been punished, or who shall be, until after the day of judgment. But those who teach that men are immortal, that, at Death, their punishment begins, tell us that after they shall have been Burned in a Blazing Hell for thousands of years, they shall be brought forth to judgment. Hence, for the plain truth as given by Peter, they have substituted just as plain a falsehood; which certainly cannot contribute to their salvation, but if, with the light before them, it be persisted in, may prove their Everlasting Destruction.

CONCLUDING PART.

Before taking leave of this subject, I shall once more endeavor to bring the reader face to face with this fiend-like production of designing apostates; and, for this purpose I shall quote a short passage from one,* the researches of whose imagination furnish an excellent example whereby to illustrate it, and show how foreign it should be to the remotest thought of a Christian, to entertain such a horrid monstrosity as the Eternal Torment of the erring of humanity in Flames of Fire and Brimstone.

Says he, while dwelling upon the unbounded expanse of the "Empire of Omnipotence," "If we would wish to acquire some definite, though imperfect, conception of the physical extent of the universe, our minds might be assisted by such illustrations as the following :—Light flies from the sun with the velocity of nearly two hundred thousand miles in a moment of time, or, about 1,400,000 times faster than the motion of a cannon ball : Suppose that one of the higher order of intelligences is endowed with a power of rapid motion superior to that of light, and with a corresponding degree of intellectual energy; that he has been flying without intermission from one province of creation to another, for six thousand years, and will continue the same rapid course for a thousand millions of years to come; it is highly probable if not absolutely certain, that, at the end of this vast tour, he would have advanced no further than the suburbs of creation—and that all the magnificent systems of material and intellectual beings he had surveyed, during his rapid flight and for such a length of ages bear no more proportion to the whole Empire of Omnipotence, than the smallest grain of sand does to all the particles of matter of the same size contained in ten thousand worlds.

---

* Thomas Dick, LL.D.

Nor need we entertain the least fear, that the idea of the extent of the Creator's power, conveyed by such a representation exceeds the bounds of reality. On the other hand it must fall almost infinitely short of it."—*Dick.*

Hence, as upon such a tour it would take a seraph, flying at the rate above mentioned, a thousand millions of years to advance no further than the suburbs of creation, a thousand millions of years would be but little more than the beginning of Eternity.

Now, just as this paragraph is so easily understood, and just as it is so positively true, just so plainly and positively is the doctrine of Eternal Burning to the effect that, if the wicked, after suffering the Torment of Burning Flames for a thousand millions of years, should, at the end of that time, cry for mercy, and say, Oh God! we have been Burning for a thousand millions of years, cannot Thy Mercy reach us now? the answer must be, No; and that ten thousand millions of years of just such Torment in Burning Flames will not end their sufferings.

According to this doctrine, as all that the seraph would see, would bear no greater proportion to the remainder than the smallest grain of sand bears to all the particles of matter of the same size contained in ten thousand worlds, so the punishment that shall be experienced by the wicked, during a thousand million of years, will bear no greater proportion to that which will follow, than one grain of sand bears to all the particles of matter of the same size contained in ten thousand worlds.

Nothing, say the advocates of this doctrine, but the Eternal Burning of the erring of humanity can meet the demand of the Almighty, and even that can never satisfy it; for they must always be Burning in Hell. O Damnable Heresy!— O Scandal against the Almighty!—not only black, but the blackest; for were it painted with the smut of hell, it could not be blacker!

But thanks to Thee, O gracious God, Who taught me this to scorn,
And turned me from night's darkest shade, to golden morn.
Thanks to Thy name, O Justice, Mercy, Love, yea, all combine,
That this, so foreign to Thyself, is that which is not mine.

Were I to make, as they have done, Thy truth to be the liar,
Oh God ! what could I then expect, what would I dare desire !
Were I to dare Thyself upbraid, with this, their charge, so dire,
No portion less would I expect, than hell's consuming fire !

TAKING LEAVE OF THE SUBJECT.

In taking leave of this subject, I wish it understood by all, that what has been said is directed against no particular creed; but against the errors herein mentioned, no matter where taught, to what extent, or by whom believed.

Furthermore, I wish it understood that, whilst fully realizing that there is nothing that comes so near the joys of heaven as a clear, clean conscience, not only do I consider the manner in which I have treated the subject of Eternal Torment in the preceding pages, as fully sanctioned by the Scriptures, and that the contents of this little volume are their unclothed realities, (as far as treated,) but that I regard this work as a fully discharged duty in behalf of the Holy Word.

And now, reader, be you who you may, my prayer to God for you is, that the light of the Gospel of the Son of God may ever shine upon your pathway, show you the difference between Inspiration, and Apostasy, and guide you to the true goal of the Christian, Eternal Life in the Everlasting Kingdom of our Lord and Saviour Jesus Christ.

INDEX.